To:

Kaetlyn

Every underdog has ~

Can't wait to see your
on the NYT best sellers!

Maddy & Cole

Vol 1:
The Food Truck Grand Prix

Written and Illustrated by
Richie Frieman

THE OMNIBUS PUBLISHING

BALTIMORE, MD

The Omnibus Publishing
5422 Ebenezer Rd.
POB 152
Baltimore, MD 21162
www.theomnibuspublishing.com

Publisher's Note: This is a work of fiction. Names, characters, places, and incidents are a product of the author's imagination. Locales and public names are sometimes used for atmospheric purposes. Any resemblance to actual people, living or dead, or to businesses, companies, events, institutions, or locales is completely coincidental.

Book Layout ©2018 - Cover Design by Richie Frieman

Ordering Information:

Quantity sales. Special discounts are available on quantity purchases by corporations, associations, and others. For details, contact the "Special Sales Department" at the address above.

Maddy & Cole / Richie Frieman. -- Vol. 1 -- 1st ed.

ISBN 978-0-9986811-5-3

For my two favorite people, Maddy and Cole.

Always dream bigger!

Love,

Daddy

Acknowledgments

I cannot say that I was the most avid reader when I was younger, especially as I struggled to find stories that spoke to me. Fortunately, I have been able to write my own stories and ever since becoming a parent I have envisioned writing something that will inspire my kids to be the best versions of themselves. I am excited to share this book with them and with you. This project as well as many of my other literary, artistic, and entrepreneurial pursuits have been challenging, and throughout all of them, I have had to overcome a disproportionate number of doubters. In spite of those who counted me out, I'm genuinely grateful for those believers and supporters who have been in my corner.

A special thank you to my manager and fellow Terp, Sammy Popat, for encouraging me to keep dreaming big while keeping me on track with this project. To Wendy Dean and The Omnibus Publishing, I am eternally grateful for you taking on this project and for publishing this book.

Your combination of patience, diligence, kindness, and energy is very rare to find. Thank you to Rosa Sophia for your editing magic and for dealing with all of my questions.

Thank you to Baltimore, the surrounding counties, and the state of Maryland, which I proudly call home, for you hold a special place in my heart. I am so grateful to belong to a community of people who rally behind each other, which is why I continue to make Baltimore the backdrop of my stories including this one.

To my parents, both biological and step, thank for you for being my cheerleaders. You can be rest assured I am putting my art degree from the University of Maryland to good use.

To my out-of-this-world, beautiful wife, thank you for making me feel like the luckiest guy in the world, day after day.

To my wonderful children, I have dedicated this book to you, because you are a daily inspiration to me, and you gave me the inspiration to write this book. Thank you for believing in me! Remember, always dream bigger, kiddos.

And, to my readers: It means so much to me that you have chosen to read my book. Thank you! This is just the beginning of our adventure together.

A Note From Maddy

Dear Friends,

Do you know what it means to be an underdog? An underdog is someone who has tremendous odds against them or an obstacle put in front of them and is thought to have no chance of succeeding. For example, in a sporting event where one team is a lot smaller than another team or maybe has a worse record, they are referred to as the underdogs. Oddly enough, being an underdog is something that some people look down upon—but they're wrong. Think about it: What does an underdog have to lose? Nothing! The underdog isn't expected to win, so if you're the underdog why not give it a shot, right? If anything, the team or person going up against the underdog should be worried. See, in any competition, there is no set winner before the event starts, and when you remember that fact, it makes it easier to understand that anyone has a chance to win. It reminds me of a saying, **"Every Underdog Has A Tale"**. I like to think this story fits that phrase perfectly.

This story is about an underdog who decided to take a chance. Did it work out as planned? Maybe, maybe not. You'll have to turn the pages to find out. However, if you believe in yourself and what's in your heart, an amazingly beautiful world will be presented to you. Sure, there will be bumps along the way, with wicked turns that hide the finish line, but that doesn't mean your goal is gone; it only means it's more challenging to find than you anticipated.

In this story, you'll meet characters who stayed on course, hung on tight when the turns came around, and despite having their own doubts, it didn't stop them from moving forward. Most importantly, they embraced their underdog identity.

With that, let's get started—shall we?

Yours truly,

Buccaneers and Cowboys

I shifted on my pillow when my dad shouted from the bottom of the steps, "Maddy Moo, time to get up!"

Ugh. Every morning at exactly 7:15, Dad wakes me up the same way.

Every. Single. Day. 7:15 on the dot, and not a minute too late.

Sure, being on time is important, but just once I'd like to stay in bed past 7:15. Oh, what it must be like to sleep until 7:16. A girl can dream.

I rubbed my eyes and tried to smooth my knotty hair with my hands.

"Maddy Moo," Dad called out again. "Munchkin Face, if you don't come down, Tucker will eat your muffins!"

Ugh, Munchkin Face? Really, Dad? Maddy Moo I've gotten used to, but Munchkin Face? I'm in the sixth grade now and I'm over the baby stuff.

Even though the temptation of delicious muffins was enough to get me out of bed, my biggest fear wasn't having to rush to get ready. I had to make sure my hyper puppy, Tucker, wouldn't eat my breakfast first. After all, Tucker would eat pretty much anything; that's what puppies do. He's not that big either, but that doesn't stop him. Tucker is a Mini-Labradoodle, which is a mix between a Labrador and a mini poodle, yet at only five months and already thirty pounds, he's hardly mini. It doesn't help that my mom and dad got him like a trillion dog toys. Tucker will only chew on my shoes laces, blankets, and table food. Someone explain that to me?

Those muffins could be gone by the time I get down there. Earlier this year, during my birthday party, Tucker ate the entire birthday cake—candles and plate included—while we opened presents in the living room. Thankfully, the candles weren't lit yet. Although, I wonder if that would have stopped him? Probably not. My dad said he has a stomach like a steel trap, whatever that means. Tucker is lucky he's cute. I don't care how goofy he is because he's mine, and I love him. There are a lot of things about me and my family that are silly, but I still love everything about us.

Any-hoo, when I woke up, my mom had already laid out my clothes—as usual. Instead of wearing what she had chosen, I decided to take care of this myself. After all, I'm in middle school now and WAAAAAAY over my mom picking out my clothes. Plus, since I was going to play at my best friend Ella's house after school that day, I needed something super sporty since she has a pirate ship themed playground and it's the coolest playground in the universe: three slides, four swings, and a trampoline. My stinky brother, Cole, and her even smellier brother, Noah, love the trampoline.

I threw on my favorite pair of jeans, which have a hole over the left knee, my favorite pink sneakers, and a purple sweatshirt with a teal peace sign in the middle. As I tied my shoes, I heard a muffled voice coming from downstairs.

"You got it, Daddy! I'm off to wescue the pwincess!"

Cole spoke in a unique way. My mom and dad said that sometimes little kids have a hard time with certain letters, and he was one of those kids. I had been helping him work on it, though.

At five years old, he thought he was a pirate who sailed the wild seas, like his favorite cartoon pirate, Buster the Buccaneer. I opened my door to find Cole standing with one hand on his hip, the other aiming a cardboard sword at my face. He brushed aside his red cape. "It's bweakfast time, Maddy! Come on. Let's go. Hustle the muscle, Moo."

"Really?" I said, narrowing my eyes. "And who's going to make me hustle, Mister?"

Cole looked at me and wrinkled his nose. "Cole will, that's who! I'm the King of the Seven Seas!" He darted between my legs and into my room, then began jumping on my bed.

"Arrrr, Maddy, my sister, wake up! It's time for bweakfast and school!" Cole leaped around my bed like a hyper spider monkey.

"Stop it, Cole! You're not a pirate! You're a little boy, so stop jumping!"

He wouldn't listen. He kept bouncing and screaming. "Arrrr, Maddy! Arrrr. Let's go, Maddy! Arrrr!"

I can usually tolerate his babyish ways for a couple of minutes, but now he was getting super annoying, and I was super-duper mad. "Stop jumping!"

Like a typical little brother, he refused to listen. "Arrrr! Arrrr!" He kept yelling, swinging his arms back and forth.

"For the last stinking time, you're not a pirate!" I shrieked. Then I yanked my blanket from underneath his feet, knocking him onto his bottom at the base of my nightstand.

Well, apparently that hurt his feelings—and his bottom—so he started crying.

Not only was I irritated about being woken up, but I would surely get in trouble if my parents knew that I'd made my brother cry.

Yikes, too late!

Dad called up from the living room. "Why is Cole crying? I heard a bang. Is everyone all right?"

I ran to the edge of the steps. "Nothing, Dad. I'll be down in a second. Cole was just helping me out of bed."

"That's not true," Cole whimpered.

Ugh, the life of a big sister is never easy.

"Come here, Cole."

"No!" he snapped, with tears on his cheeks. "You yelled at me and said I'm not a buddaneer."

"It's waaaaay too early for this drama, my man. Cole, if you come over here, I'll give you a piggyback ride down the stairs. Okay?"

A piggyback ride always made him stop crying or complaining, and he immediately forgot what was wrong in the first place. I leaned down and Cole climbed up my back, then wrapped his legs around my waist.

At first, I struggled to keep him from sliding down. "Gosh, Cole, you are getting heavy. What have you been eating?" I asked, nearly out of breath.

"Pop Pop's pancakes from his food twuck."

Straining to move, I pushed through the last three steps down the stairs. "It's truck with an R sound. Say it with me, truh-truh-truck. Pop Pop's food truck."

Cole waved his hand in the air like a cowboy. "Truck, truck, truck! Giddy-up, truck!"

"Oh boy, now you're a cowboy, too?" I moaned. "Okay then, hold on tight, partner."

It IS a Big Deal

Dad was eating breakfast at the kitchen table when Cole and I finally came roaring in.

"So nice of you to join us, Maddy Moo," Dad said in a mocking tone.

I rolled my eyes. "Yeah, yeah, yeah, I know, I know, I'm late. But I had to lug this big ol' cowboy around."

"I'm a pirate, not a cowboy," Cole said, using the table to pull himself onto his chair, allowing his little legs to dangle above the floor, swinging back and forth. "Yup, a pirate."

Oh gosh, now we're back to being a pirate?

My mom walked into the kitchen carrying our backpacks for school. "Sweetheart, don't forget after school today you're going to help on Pop Pop's food truck."

I threw my hands over my face. "Mom, you said after school we could go look at new bikes, after I play with Ella. You said if I got a good grade on my math test, which I did, and a good grade on my spelling test—which I also did—that I could get a new bike as a reward. You promised!"

She gave me a "Mom is being serious" kind of look. We all know that look, right? When moms tilt their eyebrows in, firm their lips, and stare right into you as if lasers will shoot out of their eyes. It meant bad news was on the way.

"Actually, Ella's mom texted me and said she had to switch Ella's dental appointment to after school today, so she can't play anyway. And I said we would talk about getting you a new bike, not that we would right this second. Plus, your birthday is right around the corner, and by that I don't mean tomorrow. So, you can wait a little bit."

"But Mom—"

"By the way, the bike you showed me was very expensive. Unless you're being recruited for the Tour de France, we should probably look at other bikes."

Why is my world crumbling in front of me?

"That was not the deal we had." With my hands on my hips, I climbed up on my seat for a more theatrical display.

"Deal? What deal?" Mom asked.

"The test deal."

"We're very proud of you for getting such stellar grades on your tests," she said.

"You should be proud of your hard work, Maddy," Dad added. Then he pointed at the ground. "Now, get down off your chair. Your feet don't belong on the furniture."

I grew even more aggravated, but I climbed down, keeping my hands firmly on my hips. "Daddy, talk to Mom. You guys promised!"

"I'm sorry, sweetie, but that bike is way too much," Mom replied.

"UGH, you don't understand! This is a bike like no other. The Apollo Cruiser 5200 is the best of the best in the market. It got an A+ rating and reviewers are calling it the must-have bike of the season. It's fast, sleek, cutting edge, and it's what teenagers use, Mom. Teenagers!"

Dad raised his eyebrows. "Oh gosh, Sydney," he said, glancing at my mom. "Did you hear that? Real. Live. Teenagers."

"I sense your sarcasm, Dad. You don't understand. No one understands me!" I groaned, then folded my arms on the table and put my head down. Tucker rested his chin on my lap, but even his friendly puppy greetings couldn't make me feel better. "I'll be the biggest outcast in Mt. Cedarmere – the only kid without a sweet ride. Wait, not only in our little suburb of Mt. Cedarmere, but probably even the entire city of Baltimore, which is waaaaaay bigger."

Cole tapped the back of my ponytail. "It's okay, Maddy-Moo. I understand you."

"Oh, fantastic. Cole is the only one who gets me. Him! This is my one and only ally? Someone help me."

"Plans change, sweetheart, and we can look at bikes any time," Dad said. "Plus, Pop Pop loves when you help out. He said he has a big event coming up, and your help would be greatly appreciated."

"I love the food twuck," Cole said. Then he lifted his shirt and slapped his belly. "My belly loooooooves Pop Pop's twuck too. The food twuck has the best pancakes in the world! It's Fan... um, Fantast.... It's, um...?"

"Ugh." I sighed. "It's called Pop Pop Fantastico's Fantastic Food Truck. I don't blame you, though. It's kind of a mouthful if you ask me."

I knew my tone was rather impolite but when you get aggravated you get snippy, right?

It's not that I didn't want to help; I just didn't want to on that particular day. In fact, food trucks are crazy cool. They're not like having a stand-alone restaurant your parents drag you to for family dinners, with reservations and all. See, a food truck is always on the move like a traveling circus, stopping in different places every day. Wherever there's a crowd, that's where the food trucks go. Kind of like how fishermen along the Chesapeake Bay, near our house, move around to find the best spot to catch the most fish. If one area doesn't have many fish, the fishermen continue down the shoreline until they come across an area more abundant with fish. The same thing goes for food trucks, except in this example, food trucks continue to travel down the street until they come across more hungry customers.

When people want a hot breakfast, Pop Pop parks along Pratt Street in the city, where thousands of businesspeople walk to their offices and students go to college. He sells freshly ground coffee and scrumptious pancakes, which he's known for all over the city. During lunch, he travels north to Greenspring Avenue to an office park, where a slew of people flock to the food trucks for a nice relaxing lunch outside, and he offers an array of sandwiches. Then, on most nights, Pop Pop can be found at Mt. Cedarmere Park where customers swing by for a quick bite

to eat on their way home. After all these years,
I thought Cole would finally get the name right.
I mean, Pop Pop has had that food truck since
even before my mom was born.

Sadly, Dad didn't see things the way I did. He
took a quick sip of his coffee. "Well, regardless
of whether the name is a mouthful or not, Pop
Pop's your grandfather and you should always
be happy to spend time with him. Do any of your
other friends have a cool food truck like Pop Pop
does?"

"Ha! Funny you should ask," I replied. "Allow
me to drop some knowledge on you, Daddy-O, if
you don't mind? For one thing, Pop Pop's food
truck is cool, yes... however, it's hardly fantastic.
It's rusty, old, and always has something leak-
ing under it. It needs new paint and new tires to
say the very least. And yes, I do happen to know
someone else who has a food truck, and he goes
to my school. His name is Kenny."

"Wait, isn't that the boy who put gum in your
hair, then sprinkled glitter over it?" Dad asked.

"That was mean," Cole said.

"Yeah, that's Kenny." True, he's pretty much the worst bully in school, and he acts brattier than most five-year-olds—no offense to Cole—but still, his dad has the awesomest food truck of all time.

"It was even meaner when he tripped me into a pile of mud when we were playing kick-ball in gym, but that's not the point," I added. "His dad's food truck has music, a light show from the top, and lines of people wrap around the corner like ten times wherever he shows up, whether it's morning, noon, or night. Pop Pop's truck just has...pancakes."

"And sandwiches!" Cole said.

"Fine...sandwiches, too," I grumbled.

It was obvious that my parents didn't like my improper comments about my grandfather's truck, especially because he put so much of his heart and soul into making the most delicious meals possible.

"We don't care what your friend's truck has," Mom said, "because it can't beat the history and legacy of your Pop Pop's truck." Then she glanced at Cole and used her baby voice. "Cole, you remember the story of Pop Pop's food truck, don't you?"

He nodded, grinning. "Can you tell it again, though?"

The Story of Pop Pop

My shoulders sank. "Oh, come on. Not the story about how Pop Pop came to America." I sighed, having heard it a bazillion times.

"Yes, that story," my dad replied. "That is unless, your annoying friend Kenny has a better story about his grandfather?"

I rolled my eyes.

"I love stories," Cole said.

My mom pulled my little brother onto her lap. "When your Pop Pop was about Maddy's age, he came to this country from Italy. He couldn't speak a word of English, and neither could his parents—my grandparents. His family only had twenty-three dollars in their pockets. They couldn't afford a house, so they lived on a boat that Pop Pop's father borrowed from a friend who had already moved over here. But it needed to be fixed and was just sitting in the Chesapeake Bay downtown. During the early years, they worked odd jobs to make ends meet—washing dishes in restaurants, painting houses, working as handymen, cleaning other boats in the bay, you name it. While Pop Pop was working on the docks, he would watch the other workers walk to get lunch. He could hardly afford lunch for himself, so he took the money he earned from his odd jobs, bought ingredients from a nearby bakery, and made up his own meals to sell. He then started getting a good reputation with the dock workers, who would line up for a quick meal. That's when the magic started. You've seen Pop Pop's magic chef's jacket, Cole, right?"

Again, he nodded enthusiastically.

Time out, time out! No one can deny that Pop Pop's story is remarkable—no money, a tiny broken down boat, and now he owns his own business. He went from a small operation out of a boat, to his own truck, and the truck became so popular he was able to send my mom to college. The American dream, for sure.

Yes, I'm proud of him, but how many times do I have to hear about the magic Mom always talks about? Maybe it's nice for Cole, but he's a little kid. Mom says Pop Pop has a magic apron his father wore when used to cook, and that's why his food tastes so amazing. I'm just not buying it.

"His jacket is covered in food, not magic," I quipped. "The buttons don't even match. I'm pretty sure one is an old bottle cap."

Mom glared at me. "It's that magic that allowed Pop Pop to become well-known and sustain his truck for this long. He doesn't need silly lights or special effects because he has a magic apron, delicate hands, and an imagination to win customers over."

"Look, I get it. I do." I chewed on a piece of my muffin. "But—"

"You know, Maddy, if you don't like his truck, then I'm sure Pop Pop wouldn't mind if you helped him fix it up. That is, if you feel it's in such desperate need of help."

Dad's eyes widened, then he snapped his fingers. "I've got an idea!"

"I like ideas," I said.

"Maybe you could work with him, make some money—just the way he did—and save up for your bike."

I nodded slowly. "Keep talking, keep talking. I'm listening."

"I'll make the deal even better." He scratched his chin as he thought. "If you convince Pop Pop to pay you to work for him, then Mom and I will match whatever he pays you, dollar for dollar. So, if he pays you twenty-five dollars, I'll throw in another twenty-five on top of it. The more you work, the more you earn, just as Pop Pop did when he was your age."

"Good idea, Reed!" Mom said to Dad. "Why don't you do that, Maddy? You're a great artist and very crafty. Remember when you helped me pick out all those decorations for our July Fourth party? All I did was pay for the decorations, but you did all the work."

"Or the time you helped me redo my office upstairs," Dad said. "It was nothing but blank white walls and you picked out great colors, helped me frame some photos, and even found a cool desk for me online."

"Maybe he'll hire you as his decorator," Mom added.

"A decorator?" I asked.

"You know, like those makeover shows on TV. I'm sure Pop Pop has a budget—nothing you can't work with, though," Dad said.

"I'm going to need a pretty big budget for that hunk of junk."

Cole took his shirt off and held it in the air, whipping it around his head as if he was a pirate wielding a sword. "I want to help, too. I can be the pancake tester and eat them across the seven seas!"

Cole getting super excited always made my parents laugh. "Okay, okay—Buster the Buccaneer and Maddy the Decorator, it is. Now put your clothes back on, silly boy. It's time for school."

School's Got Me Like...

Ever since I was in kindergarten, my mom has been dropping me off at school on her way to work. In kindergarten and first grade it was acceptable, but now I'm in middle school—the big leagues. Doesn't she understand what it means to be in middle school? I mean, I am so close to being an adult. I didn't want to be treated the way Cole was when he went to daycare.

Still, despite my age and maturity level, my mom always yelled out the window, "Have a great day, sweetheart!" The whole school could hear her.

Ugh, so embarrassing. She might as well blab it over the morning announcements. As we arrived, I sank down into my seat, trying to hide from the loud baby music Cole listened to as it blasted through the speakers.

"Can't we listen to the normal radio like everyone else, Mom?" I begged. "Why do we have to listen to Cole's stupid cartoon music?"

"Maddy said stupid!" Cole shouted. "You can't say stupid! That's a bad word. Maddy said a bad word! Mommy, Maddy said stupid."

"You're right, Cole. Stupid is a bad word," Mom said. "Say you're sorry to your brother, Maddy."

"Fine. Whatever. I'm sorry. I still don't like his music."

"Okay, maybe tomorrow you can listen to your music. We can share. Sound good, Cole?"

Cole smiled and gave a thumbs up.

As I reached for the door, my mom spoke in a sing-song voice. "Have a good day, honey, and don't forget about going to see Pop Pop after school."

My shoulders sank. "I know, I know. The food truck. Whoop-dee-doo."

I was halfway out of the car when I felt a hand on my backpack. It was Cole reaching out and holding onto one of the key chains on my zipper. I turned around to see him blowing me a kiss with his other hand.

"You're my best friend, Maddy. You know that? I love you," he said.

Even though Cole was difficult at times—okay, a lot of the time—I still loved him. Plus, when you're a big sister, you have to make sure your younger siblings know you care. That's Big Sister 101. It's the first lesson you learn.

"You're my best friend too, buddy," I said. "Be good at school today for Mrs. JoAnn."

"Aw, that's so sweet, you guys," Mom cooed, as if my kindness toward Cole was some sort of victory for her.

Then, just as I got out of the car, a loud screech that could have been heard two towns over came from the front of the school. "MAAAADDY!"

It was my real best friend, Ella, waiting for me the same way she'd been doing every day since kindergarten. Ella and I live on the same street and have been besties since we were babies. We were even born on the same day—the fifteenth—but I'm a month older. Our moms used to push us around the neighborhood in strollers together. I mean, that kind of makes us like sisters, more than best friends if you think about it. Well, sisters who don't really resemble one another. While my hair is light brown, kind of wavy, and hangs down to the middle of my back, Ella has a dark chocolate bob matching her cocoa bean colored eyes. I'm also a bit taller than Ella, but don't let her little frame fool you because she is super-duper strong thanks to spending eight hours a week in gymnastics classes. My dad jokes around that she's stronger than most teenage boys. So, once again, Ella will be going as an Olympic gymnast for Halloween in a couple of weeks, making that the third year in a row. I'll be going as a zombie lacrosse player with fake blood and a ripped jersey, along with a lacrosse stick that has an ax head on the bottom. And just as Ella and I have been together since the stroller days, she's here at school waiting for me.

"Hi, Ella! I'll be there in a second." I turned to my mom. "Bye, Mom. Bye, Coley. See you later." Then I ran across the yard and toward the school to meet Ella.

Ella and I walked into school and toward our lockers to hang up our jackets and put our backpacks away before homeroom. In our school, homeroom is the central meeting place for our class, even though we separate throughout the day based on different schedules. Ella is normally talkative and excited, but today she was talking faster than ever.

"O-M-G, Maddy. O-M-G, O-M-G, O...M...G!"

"Slow down, slow down. O-M-G, what?"

"Look at what Kenny handed out this morning." Ella showed me a bright orange cupcake with a giant blob of white icing on top, just in time for Halloween. "These are so delicious!" She took a bite. "Here, I saved one for you." She handed me a similar orange cupcake, but mine had yellow sprinkles on top.

I took a bite. "Wow, this cupcake is out of this world!"

"I know, right? Kenny told me his dad will be selling them as a new dessert for his dad's burger truck at the Charm City Food Truck Grand Prix this weekend."

"The what?" I said, still stuffing my face with cupcake goodness.

"Maddy, there have been flyers all over the school about it."

I shook my head, still munching on the cupcake.

"Gosh. I swear, Maddy Moo, sometimes you boggle the mind." Ella handed me a folded piece of paper. "Excuse the drawings all over it, but Noah was scribbling on it in the car. Some five year olds can't understand what "please don't draw on my paper" means. But all he draws is circles, anyway, so just read around them."

I unfolded the paper.

THE INAUGURAL CHARM CITY FOOD TRUCK GRAND PRIX.

Food trucks from all over the city competing for a one day event to crown the best food truck in Charm City.

"This must be why Pop Pop needs our help today."

"Wait, your Pop Pop will have his food truck there, too?" Ella asked.

We both read over the paper for the details. Then we saw the biggest surprise of all.

"Ella, do you see this?" I said, my eyes widening. It was in bold letters at the bottom of the page. "It says here the grand prize of the Grand Prix will be $1,000!"

"I've never seen so many zeroes before."

"That's right, Ella. One thousand big ones!"

I freeze reading the numbers out loud a second time. It's a habit of mine whenever I find myself at a loss for words.

Ella tapped me on the shoulder.

"Um, hellooooo. Is anyone home? Wake up, Maddy!"

I was still speechless, too busy trying to figure out what I would do with one thousand dollars. I started to make a mental list:

1. A new computer, like the ones spies use in the movies, so I can control my army of robots that do all of my chores.

2. A new telescope that I could use to see aliens having dinner on Mars.

3. A new wardrobe consisting of only lacrosse shorts, basketball jerseys, and sneakers.

4. A pair of hydraulic shoes that could help me slam dunk over a pile of cars as if I had super powers.

5. A remote control that allows me to mute Cole at any time.

6. A waterbed for Tucker that's fit for the king that he is.

7. A surfboard that turns into a motorboat at the flip of a switch.

8. A full-size dinosaur skeleton like the ones from the museum to keep in the front yard.
9. Front row tickets to the NBA and NFL Super Bowl every year for the rest of my life.

Then I realized I was missing one.

10. A new bike! If I had a thousand dollars, I could get a new bike!

Heck, I could get the whole entire school new bikes at that point. I would be like a talk show host giving away a new car to her studio audience. "You get a bike, and you get a bike, and you get a bike...."

The list could go on forever, but after the bike there was no reason to think about anything else. I would be the Queen of Mt. Cedarmere Middle School, and I'd have people fan me whenever I felt tired and carry me through the halls on a giant throne.

Oh, it will be luxurious!

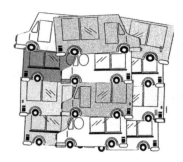

One Thousand Smackaroonies

Ella clapped her hands loudly to get me out of my dreamlike haze. "Maddy, when you doze off sometimes it's hard to get you back."

"Ella, do you know what this means?"

"What, what means?"

"What one thousand dollars means."

"Oh, that! Um, no. What's it mean?"

"It means that if I win the Grand Prix, then I could finally buy the bike I want."

"Now you're talking!"

"Ella, that's one thousand smackaroonies! That's life-changing money. That's.... That's....

That's.... Uh-oh, I'm going to faint. Catch me, Ella," I said, throwing my arm across my forehead.

Sure, I was being a little over-the-top, but I was unable to grasp the concept of so much money, so I fell lifelessly into Ella's arms.

She started to bring me back to Earth by slapping my cheeks. "Okay, okay, okay, Miss Drama Queen, why don't you wake up already?"

"Imagine it, Ella," I said again.

"That would be legendary, Maddy."

I sat up and grabbed her by the shoulders, "Ella, I have to help Pop Pop win the Grand Prix."

For once, she wasn't completely on board with me. "I don't know, Maddy. It's not that easy. There are a lot of food trucks out there. I mean, look at this. It says there will be over fifty trucks competing for the grand prize of one thousand dollars. Kenny's dad will be there, too. Talk about some steep competition."

Where was that good ole fashioned confidence boost that I needed from Ella—especially in a time like this?

I read down the list of vendors. Each name felt like an icy snowball striking me in the face, each one stinging more than the last. "Ella, you're right. These are the best in town. The best of the best."

I began reading out loud from the list. "Phil and Monica's Burrito Barn, Michelle and Craig's Super Salad Mobile, Joyce and Tim's Ice Cream Castle, Felicia and Mark's SoCal Smoothie Car, Adam's Steak Station…"

I had to stop because it was getting too depressing. "Oh, Ella, how on earth can Pop Pop win? This is so awful."

My plan was over. At number four on the list, my dream was fading away, but once I reached number ten, the bike had not only disappeared but my legs felt like rubber. At this point, how could I even ride a bike?

"No offense," Ella began, "but even though your Pop Pop makes the most delicious pancakes ever, his truck isn't very appetizing. No pun intended."

I leaned against the lockers and slumped down, knowing she was right.

"Oh, come on, Maddy, there's always next year for him. Maybe you can start to prepare and then focus on that for a big win."

I knew she was trying to be nice, but her advice wasn't helping. "Next year? I can't wait until next year for a bike," I whined.

We sat silently for a few minutes. Then the bell rang loudly throughout the hallway, letting students know homeroom was starting. The halls went from jam-packed to empty as kids scattered to their classes. "Come on, Maddy, you can't sit in the hall forever. We'll be late!"

I held out my hand. "Please help me up. I don't have any energy left. Self-doubt and loneliness are my only friends. Maybe you should just leave me here to wallow in my misery. Save yourself, Ella. Save yourself!"

She leaped to her feet. "Come on, come on, you lazy bum. Up and at 'em."

The Attack of Kenny and Walter

I'm usually in good spirits when I arrive at homeroom. I love school. I mean, I seriously love it, probably more than anyone else. Mt. Cedarmere Middle School has been around for fifty years and most of my family members walked through the same halls when they were my age. I even have the same locker that my Uncle Brad used when he was in sixth grade. Even the teachers are amazing, especially my favorite, Mrs. Mechak, who happens to be my homeroom teacher as well.

Mrs. Mechak is incredibly smart, too, and she only graduated college a few years ago. She's much younger than the other teachers in the school, and she likes a lot of the same music as we do. The other teachers look like my mom, dad, or even Pop Pop. Mrs. Mechak also has impeccable fashion sense. Every day she wears a fabulous necklace to match her bright pink bracelets, one on each arm. She's very creative, too. Each holiday she turns her classroom into a magical wonderland. Since Halloween was right around the corner, the classroom was decorated with spooky goblins, fake spider webs, and a dozen mini pumpkins on Mrs. Mechak's desk. She'd even rigged our classroom door to make the noise of a rusty old door whenever it was opened, as if something might jump out of the shadows like in a horror movie. She also dyed her chocolate brown hair green so she looked like a witch. That's right, a teacher with green hair.

The very coolest part about Mrs. Mechak is her pet chameleon, Shades, who lives in a three foot long tank on a bookshelf behind her desk. Surrounding the tank are many books to choose from, each spine a different color so the shelves of books make up a rainbow. The shelves are over-flowing, and Mrs. Mechak has so many books that she lets us borrow any book we want for as long as we like. We can take as many as we want, but in return we have to do one good deed—like helping a friend or cleaning the chalkboard eras-ers. That's actually my favorite thing to do.

One time, when I was on eraser duty with Ella, we clapped off so much chalk dust that our hair was covered in chalk flakes. We walked around the rest of the day pretending we were pink and green ghosts.

Today Mrs. Mechak was standing beside her desk with a marble notebook in her hand, when we walked in. "Good morning, Maddy and Ella," she said enthusiastically.

"It's hardly a good morning, Mrs. Mechak."

"Really? What seems to be the problem, Maddy?" she asked, her tone showing her concern.

I dragged my feet as if they had chains on them. "Oh, nothing," I moaned.

"It's a long story," Ella said.

"Long or short," she began, "if you need someone to talk to, I'm always here for you."

"Thanks, Mrs. Mechak. I appreciate it," I mumbled. "But unless you are a real witch with real powers that can turn my world back to normal, I don't think you can help."

I started walking to my seat when Kenny greeted me in the unfiltered, disgusting style he always uses. He was like a vulture on a rooftop seeking prey. He leaned against the classroom windowsill with Walter, both of them surveying the entire classroom for potential targets. Sadly, I'm their favorite. Lucky me!

"Hey, Maddy, Halloween isn't until the end of October. What's with the goblin costume?" he blared, while the other kids in the classroom laughed.

"Yeah, a nerdy goblin," Walter added.

"Kenny, Walter!" Mrs. Mechak snapped. "Is that the way we talk to our classmates? Why would you say that? Apologize right now."

Her tone caused them both to straighten where they stood, standing away from the windowsill.

In unison, they said, "Sorry." But it was so faint and weak. I knew they didn't mean it.

"Don't listen to them, Maddy," Ella said.

"I'm just happy they sit on the other side of the room. The farther away from them, the better."

As we made our way down the aisle, Kenny took another chance to showcase how rude he was. "Or as your little brother would say, 'I'm sawwy,'" he added, mocking the way Cole talks.

"Kenny, one day Cole will talk perfectly fine, but forever you will be the worst kid in the school!" I told him, letting my anger get the best of me and drawing stares from the other classmates.

"Kenny, what did I just say?" Mrs. Mechak interjected. "You and Walter will be seeing me during the afternoon break instead of going outside like the rest of the class."

Both boys then sat down in their seats, shooting evil looks my way.

There are fifteen kids in my class, including me, with our desks in three rows of five. I'm in the same row with Ella, and she's the row leader, which means she gets to take attendance for our row. Of all the jobs to have in the classroom, be-ing row leader is a sweet gig. We rotate jobs every week and this week, I'm the trash helper, which is the opposite of sweet. It's sooooo not fun.

We opened our notebooks, as we did every morning, and began to work on the assignment that Mrs. Mechak wrote on the board. Each morning she had a short assignment for us. She says it's supposed to "jump-start our brains", but my brain needed more than a jump-start, espe-cially after seeing the topic: "What are you excit-ed about for the upcoming weekend?"

Just what I wanted to talk about, right? It's as if someone was torturing me. Ugh, I bet it's Kenny. How could I possibly have anything posi-tive to write about?

Mrs. Mechak tapped her pencil on the end of her wooden desk to get our attention. I felt like I needed a crane to lift my head up, but somehow I managed.

"Class, take your time and think hard," she said. "Remember, there is no one right answer. Everyone has a chance to express themselves and everyone's ideas are equally unique. Keep in mind, just because someone's plans may appear to be a bit more exciting than your own, it's not about what you do, but how you do it. You may talk quietly amongst yourselves as long as the work gets completed, but please be respectful to those around you." She put on her glasses and sat back down behind her desk.

I stared at my paper, wondering what I should be excited about. Oh, that's right—nothing! Silly me for even trying. Ella turned to face me. "Maddy, did you hear what Mrs. Mechak said?"

"Uh, yeah, I've been here the entire time."

"And?"

"And what, Ella?"

"She makes a good point."

"About what? You're losing me fast, my dear, and frankly I have little steam left in this engine, so if you have a point, I suggest you put your thoughts into overdrive."

"About plans for this weekend and how everyone's are different and no one person's idea of fun is better than another's."

Sometimes I wonder if Ella and I even speak the same language.

I didn't answer because I had no idea what she was talking about, so I did what anyone else would've done in my position: I stared at her with my brow crinkling.

"Maddy, I have an idea." She spoke in a loud whisper—the kind of tone in which someone tries to speak softly, but it doesn't work out that way. Ella hadn't quite grasped the concept of talking so no one else could hear her. A couple students turned to glance in our direction.

I slapped my cheeks, trying to bring myself back to life. "You know, Ella, right now I feel as if my brain is sinking into a pile of quicksand. To that point, my hyperactive best friend, who I love dearly but now feel as if we've never met before, I beg you to speed it up."

"This will change the entire outcome of your weekend."

"Really? Does it involve convincing Kenny's dad and dozens of other food truck owners to not enter the competition? Because that's the only good idea I can come up with."

"No, silly. What if you actually won the competition?"

Gotta love best friends, right? Here I am on the brink of a nervous breakdown and Ella asks me what it would be like if we won the Grand Prix.

"Is that your bright idea?" I said, my tone betraying my annoyance.

Ella nodded proudly.

"Okay, I'll play. What if, instead of it snowing ten inches this winter, it snowed candy corn? Or what if Tucker could play the clarinet? Or what if Cole became a real pirate?" I threw my hands up in frustration. "Come on, Ella, we just went over this. You said it yourself, there are sooooo many food trucks, and there's no way we can win."

"Listen. It's like this assignment, okay? Everyone's weekend is different and everyone is unique. The contest isn't just about one type of food, it's about all kinds of food! There's no rule that says one type of food is better than another. It's all up to interpretation, and it's an even playing field. It all comes down to how good the food is, right?"

I groaned. "I'm still not feeling ya, El," I said, my eyes half-closed in exhaustion.

"Sure, Kenny's food truck is crazy awesome, and Avery's Juice Bar has the best smoothies—and milkshakes, for that matter—but the contest is for anyone."

"And?"

"And, silly, that means anyone can win."

"I'm sorry. I still don't get it!"

Mrs. Mechak heard my outburst and said, "Is there a problem, girls?"

"No, Mrs. Mechak."

Ella leaned in closer and whispered, "You are so difficult, Maddy. It's like what my mom said when I was nervous about starting gymnastics: Everyone has an equal chance to be great. You just have to try. If you don't try, you'll never know. Your Pop Pop has the best pancakes. That alone could make him win. You just have to make everyone talk about the pancakes, and not the food at the other trucks."

"I don't know. That's easy to say but nearly impossible to do."

She crossed her arms and rolled her eyes. "Fine, don't try. Buy a ticket and watch all those other trucks—each of whom think he or she can win and are willing to try—fight for the prize, while you sit back and collect dust for another year on the shelf of loneliness."

"The shelf of loneliness? Really, Ella?"

"I call it as I see it, and right now everyone is preparing for the big win except you and your Pop Pop. You must try, Maddy. You have to, or it's back on that ole shelf."

She turned around to finish her assignment. I thought about what she'd said and even though my stubbornness can get the best of me at times, I saw what she meant. Haunted by the "what if" factor, my brain did a back-flip.

If I don't try, I'll never know.

I'll always wonder "what if" and "why not?"

What if we tried our hardest and actually won?

Why not our truck?

Why not my wish?

CRAZIER THINGS HAVE HAPPENED THAN HAVING MY DREAMS COME TRUE.

I tapped my pencil on the blank paper, trying to figure out how to illustrate my thoughts. I stared at the paper, and it stared right back at me. My art teacher, Mr. Anthony, always said, "For an artist, the scariest and the most exciting thing is to face a blank canvas. Some will see fear, and others will see freedom." Like all the great artists before me, it was my time to face my doubts. It began with Mrs. Mechak's assignment.

As if a switch had been flipped inside my body, my nerves settled, and everything made sense. I finally knew what I was excited about! I began jotting down notes with an abundance of energy.

Ella heard me shuffling through a stack of colored pencils and drawing faster than the wind rushing through my hair as I rode the new bike my winnings would bring.

"A few more minutes, class," Mrs. Mechak said.

I remained focused on my paper.

"Maddy, what are you doing?" Ella asked.

I was so focused on my drawing that I didn't respond.

"Maddy," she said again. "What are you doing?"

I finished, stood up, and slammed the piece of paper on Ella's desk. "Boom! Here it is."

She hesitantly picked up my paper. "Six Days To $1K," she read. "What does that mean?"

"That's the symbol for a thousand—as in a thousand dollars—and Saturday is six days, including today. And come Saturday, Pop Pop and I will win that money, honey!"

New Bike Dreams

For the rest of the day, time seemed to move at a glacial pace, the clock ticking slower and slower with every second. I know my daily routine like the back of my hand, which made anticipating the end of the school day even more agonizing. After we left homeroom, I had science class with Mr. Joseph, then gym with Mrs. Benjamin, over to Mr. Anthony for art, lunch, then back to Mrs. Mechak for History and English. Watching the time pass was worse than watching paint dry. It got so bad that I even asked Mrs. Mechak if the clock was working properly.

"Of course it is, Maddy," she said. "I actually changed the batteries last week."

I couldn't sit still and couldn't stop thinking about all the ideas for Pop Pop's truck. New paint, menu options, decorations, new signage to draw people in—the possibilities were endless.

Like Mom said, "Maddy, your artistic talents can transform his food truck into the greatest food truck there ever was."

After an agonizingly long day, the bell rang to signal school was over, and I bolted out the door as if I my feet were on fire and the hallway was a giant swimming pool. I ran past the office, through the cafeteria, and barreled through the main door in front of the school to wait for my mom. Yes, me, Maddy, was anxiously waiting for Mom to pick me up. That's the first time that's happened since I was in daycare. I jumped up and down like Cole does when he has to go potty because I just couldn't contain my energy, and not because I actually had to go to the bathroom—just needed to make that part clear. After school, I usually hang out with Ella on the open fields alongside the carpool line playing soccer (she insists on being the goalie) or making string bracelets on the benches by the carpool line, while we wait to be picked up. Today, however, I don't have time for games. Today, I am all business! I am on a mission.

When my mom pulled up, Cole sat strapped into his car seat looking through a *Buster the Buccaneer* comic book. He doesn't know how to read, but he likes the pictures. My mom didn't even have time to get out of the car to help me in. I beat her to it.

"All set, Mom. Let's go help Pop Pop," I said.

"Wow, Maddy, you sure changed your tune. When I dropped you off, you were dreading it."

"What can I say? I'm a changed woman. Now less talking, more driving, Momma."

"I'm going to help Pop Pop, too!" Cole said, clapping his hands. "I brought him one my favorite comics since I know how much he likes them."

"Ugh, really? What can you do? You can't even eat without spilling on yourself," I said, feeling irritated. After all, I had a lot on the line here. I couldn't put up with Cole's immature antics getting in the way of my success.

"I can too help! Mommy, tell Maddy I can help, too," he wailed.

Mom adjusted the mirror and glared at us. "Cole can be very helpful...in his own way. We'll all pitch in. I used to work for Pop Pop all the time and when your dad and I started dating in college, he even helped Pop Pop in the summer."

"Can you please not talk about you two dating? I still have my lunch in me."

"It's true, though. We had a blast."

"You did?" I asked.

"Of course. I loved it. Everyone did. Me, Aunt Jill, Uncle Brad, Uncle Matt...everyone worked there. In fact, by the time I was your age, I was taking orders, making sandwiches, you name it. That truck is more than just a food truck. It's a family tradition and something we all take pride in."

"You were like a real chef?" I asked, surprised to hear that my mom was working with Pop Pop on the grill when she was a little girl.

She laughed. "I guess I was, in a way, but nothing like your famous Pop Pop."

"Wow, I didn't know kids could be full-blown chefs."

"Well, not a real chef. Real chefs spend years studying their craft, and most go to culinary school. It's a college for chefs. I was more of a sous-chef."

"What's a sous-chef?"

"It's like an assistant to the head chef," Mom explained as she slowed at a traffic light. "Or someone who is studying under a master chef. In this case, that's Pop Pop. Being a chef is very serious business, and when you're younger, you have to make sure an adult is always around. You can never use knives or be around the hot stoves or meals. You must always be careful. I didn't touch anything that involved the stove until I was a teenager. It's actually a law," she added. "Still, everyone has to start somewhere—just like Pop Pop did—and in the beginning, it's not always easy. Being a chef like Pop Pop is not like making peanut butter and jelly sandwiches at home. What he does is..." She paused to find the right word. "It's more like magic, Maddy."

I had heard about his magic for so long, and doubted its merit, but now, I needed to believe in it if we were going to win.

My mom smiled into the rearview mirror. "Yup, magic. What Pop Pop does with food is truly magical. There's much more to his food truck than the food he creates. You'll see. Trust me."

Interesting. I pulled out my phone and quickly texted Ella, I got this thing in the bag, baby! Pop Pop has a very magical surprise that will surely make us win.

I slid my phone back into my bag and smiled out the window, feeling optimistic and dreaming of the new bike I would get with my winnings.

Magic Like You've Never, Ever Seen Before

A t about four-thirty, we arrived at the Mt. Cedarmere Business Park where dozens of food trucks gathered in the parking lot, setting up for the dinner rush that usually started ar ound five-thirty. The prime food truck spots, located by the park entrance, are the best since they're the first trucks customers see. Pop Pop is always early.

Pop Pop's truck was next to a line of gorgeous autumn trees filled with yellow, orange, and red leaves. Cole and I love autumn more than any other time of year. Cole has a habit of sneaking leaves from the playground at school into his backpack and saving them in an old shoe box under his bed. He once told me, "I'm trying to grow my own tree, Maddy." When I reminded him that's not how it works, he started to cry, so I dropped the subject. However, his thought process is kind of imaginative and every now and then I'll donate a few leaves to his collection. Mom parked behind Pop Pop's food truck alongside the back door, which was wide open. We could see Pop Pop working diligently inside at the grill.

I leaped out of the car. "Hey, Cole, there are some good leaves for you to collect over here. Look at all the colors!"

He couldn't wait to grab some while he waited for Mom to unbuckle him. "Mommy, Mommy! Leaves, look at the leaves! Hurry, quick, unbuckle me!"

"Don't worry, there will be plenty of leaves for you. Let me get you out. I'm sure Pop Pop has a bag we can put them in."

I leaned over and took his hand. "Coley, don't play with your buckles. You have to wait for

Mommy. Remember, we have to be careful because there are so many cars here today and a lot of people running around trying to get dinner."

Cole sank back into his car seat. "I just get so excited!"

I laughed. "I know you do, Cole."

I was excited, too. Today, we would start getting Pop Pop in gear for the Grand Prix. We were just about to grab a handful of canary yellow leaves for Cole, when a familiar voice sang from the side of Pop Pop's truck.

"I *miei amori*," Pop Pop shouted. That's Italian for my loves. Pop Pop mixes Italian with English a lot.

"Ah, my loves! My angels! My little snack treats. It's you, it's you! Come to Pop Pop Fantastico! I have missed you all so, so, so much." He bent down, his arms wide open, clad in his standard chef's attire—a denim button-down shirt, bright madras pants, and an emerald green chef's jacket, with eight mix-matched buttons down the middle. He also wore a baseball cap that displayed his food truck's logo, his thick curls of gray hair hidden beneath.

We shouted, "Pop Pop!" as we ran to him.

He lifted both of us in one swoop, holding us close with his meaty arms, kissing our cheeks as if he hadn't seen us in years when it had only been last week.

"A kiss for you," he said, kissing Cole's cheek again. "And a kiss for you, dear," he said, kissing mine. His fuzzy mustache tickled our faces as we squirmed in his arms.

"Pop Pop, that tickles!" I cried out in laughter.

"Pop Pop, your mustache is pwickly like Velcwo," Cole said.

"It's prickly like V-V-V-Velcro, Cole," I said, correcting him.

"Ah, it's all the same to me. See, Coley, Pop Pop Fantastico still can't say certain words right either sometimes. Don't worry, you'll get it, *mi tesoro.*"

That's Italian for my treasure.

Pop Pop let us down softly, then leaned over to Mom to kiss her on the cheek. "Ah, my sweetie,

I'm so happy you all came to help me," he said, stepping back and placing his hands on his hips. "All day long, I make delicious food, but this..." He opened his arms wide, gesturing to the three of us. "This is my greatest creation ever. Okay, who's hungry?" Pop Pop had a delicious selection of pastries ready for us, and we all dug in.

I grabbed a cheese croissant and took a big bite. "Pop Pop, is it true?" I asked.

"Is what true, my dear?"

"The magic! Your magic, the magical truck, and the magical food. You have magic that can make amazing things happen in the kitchen. Tell me this is true."

Pop Pop leaned close, so close his nose touched mine, and then he wiggled it back and forth. "Maddy, my love, it is true. Magic like you've never, ever seen before."

LOST:
MADDY'S HOPES
AND DREAMS.
☹
IF FOUND, PLEASE
RETURN TO MADDY ASAP!

Magic Shmadrick

"Here, take my hands, kids, and let's walk inside Pop Pop Fantastico's Fantastic Food Truck."

It had been a while since I'd witnessed his food truck in action. I usually saw it parked in his driveway during off hours. Usually I'm in school or sleeping while he's working in the early mornings. As we snacked on some of Pop Pop's homemade treats, we noticed the other food trucks coming in as well. It was one thing to look at the list of food trucks on paper, but seeing the variety of food trucks in person was another story. Paulina's Perfect Pizza truck pulled up and parked. It had a giant metal pizza on the roof, shining with neon lights. Next to that was Carlo's Cookie Truck with one of the bakers wearing a chocolate chip cookie costume. Kenny's dad's truck pulled up, too. Even before he parked, people were already waiting to place an order.

The more I looked around, the more amazing trucks I saw, and each was shinier than the next. But there was something very different about Pop Pop's truck. Unlike the others, his looked weathered and beat up from time, and surely needed a trip—or two or three—to the mechanic. Carlo's truck, on the other hand, was bright white with small cookies painted all over it and the name Carlo spelled in chocolate chips.

Pop Pop's truck had nothing decorative on it at all. Other trucks were covered with cool artwork, like Rowan's Maryland Crab Cake Caravan, which featured a photo of her juggling three orange crabs in the air. Pop Pop's only had the letters of Fantastico's Fantastic Food Truck peeling off and faded from the sun. His tires were nearly bald and only two of them had hubcaps.

Still more trucks, like Tina's Tacos, had clean tires that looked like they could go through a foot of snow with ease. I doubted Pop Pop's could make it through a pile of leaves. Also, his windows were dusty and covered with old stickers, while everyone else had crystal clear windows shining in the sun. Looking at all the other trucks was an enlightening experience...and not in a good way.

If Pop Pop has magic, when does he plan to use it? I would have whipped out my magic a long time ago if I were him.

Just when I thought I couldn't become any more doubtful about Pop Pop's food truck, I heard a familiar, whiny voice call my name. "Hey, Maddy!"

When I turned around, I saw Kenny, my sworn enemy, the meanest of the mean, taunting and mocking me from the window of his dad's truck as he turned past Pop Pop's truck to find a spot of his own. "Check out my dad's awesome food truck!" he shouted. "Can your truck even move? Let me know if you need a tow back to town." Then he burst into laughter.

"Just ignore him," Mom said, putting her arm around me.

Pop Pop heard him as well. "The only big mouths I care about are the ones with big stomachs to match," he added. "Don't listen to that boy."

"Trust me, I try not to, but sadly he's around me at school all day, every day," I muttered. "Now, I have to see him here, too?"

I leaned against the side of the truck and continued to watch the other trucks pull in, set up, and begin to operate. I went from an extreme level of confidence to feeling absolutely miserable. I took a deep breath and shook my head as I realized the truth, *there's no way we can win.*

Incoming Ninja

The realization that Pop Pop's food truck was not fantastic at all crushed my dreams of winning the Grand Prix and getting my new bike. How on earth could we win when Pop Pop's truck looks so old and beaten up? As far as the "magic," I seriously doubted it would work and questioned whether he even had any at all. The greatest magician in the world turning Cole into a fire-breathing dragon seemed easier than what would be needed to make Pop Pop's truck a winner in the Grand Prix. In fact, we would need a team of magicians. No, an army of them. Wait, make that an entire world of magicians, each with their own army, to help turn Pop Pop's disgusting hunk of junk into anything remotely presentable.

I couldn't take it any longer.

I felt defeated.

I moved from the side of the truck and sat down next to a large oak tree that was beginning to lose its crimson leaves. Wrapped my arms around my legs I buried my head into my knees.

Mom noticed me sitting by myself. "Is there something wrong, dear?"

I looked up, knowing she'd see the sadness in my eyes. "No, Mom. It's....I'm just not feeling well." I couldn't tell her the truth.

"Would you like to leave?"

Cole sat giggling with Pop Pop as he cleaned the counter of his food truck window, then helped place napkins and forks in plastic baskets for customers. I didn't have it in me to tell him how distraught I was. I'm sure my face showed it, though. I couldn't tell Pop Pop what I was thinking: "Hey, your food truck is nothing but scrap metal on wheels." I thought it, and I felt it, but saying it out loud would be insanely rude.

Why wasn't Pop Pop upset by how amazing all the other food trucks were in comparison to his? What was I missing? Why doesn't he see what I see?

"Maddy, would you like to go home?" Mom asked again.

I sighed deeply. "No, that's okay. I know Cole is having fun. Is it okay if I lie down in the car and take a nap?"

"Sure. There's a blanket in the back seat if you need it."

I walked over to my mom's car, slipped in, and wrapped myself in her thick wool blanket. I watched Pop Pop and Cole from the car window. I was having a miserable time, but Pop Pop was prepping an excited Cole for the big night, making sure everything was organized and neatly presented. Rather than participating, I sulked and watched. "Coley, my little boy, come help Pop Pop Fantastico set up. We're going to have a long line tonight! I have a special present for you, too."

"For me?" Cole gasped. "What is it, what is it, what is it?"

Pop Pop handed him a green chef's jacket with bronze buttons down the middle, just like the one Pop Pop wears, along with a ball cap that read "Fantastico's" in green. Pop Pop handed Cole a little step stool, as well, to allow him to see over the counter.

"Here, my boy. This is your official chef's coat. See, every chef must wear a jacket like this—long sleeves, double-breasted, and high on the neck, so nothing touches your skin. After all, you don't want to spill anything on you or mess up your clothes, right? Some jackets are white, gray, or black, but I like green. Green is my favorite color."

Cole stuck his chin in the air and said, "Mommy, look what Pop Pop gave me! I'm a serious chef now, Mommy."

Pop Pop patted him on the back. "Now, Cole, this jacket is not just a chef's jacket. It's a magic chef's jacket." He slapped his chest with both hands. "See, like mine. Magic, my boy!"

Cole's eyes nearly leaped off his face. "Nooooo way! Really? A magical chef's jacket?"

"Ah, yes way, my grandson. A magical jacket. When you put this jacket on, and when I wear mine, magic happens. Magic like you've never seen! And look—there's your name, too."

Cole appeared to be so busy admiring his new chef's jacket that he missed his own name on the left side written in gold. "Mommy! Mommy!" he shouted. "Pop Pop gave me a magical chef's jacket, and it has my name on it!"

"That's adorable, Cole. You know, I had one when I was little, too. But yours is way nicer."

"I have one for Maddy, as well," Pop Pop said. "Sydney, have you seen Maddy?" He turned to Mom. "Where did she go?"

I watched him look around for me and when his gaze caught mine, I sat slumped in the car seat. I didn't want him to see me cry.

"Oh, she's not feeling well right now, Dad. She's taking a nap."

Pop Pop waved to me. "Feel better, Maddy. I have a present for you when you're ready."

I gave him a small wave.

Even though I couldn't see Pop Pop's face from my seat, I was able to look through the open back door and watch him teach Cole about becoming a chef. They were at the front window where he served customers and took their orders.

"In this fridge, I keep all the cold food items. We can never leave the door open or else the food will go bad. Air is our enemy, Cole."

"Got it. Air is da bad guy, Pop Pop."

"And over here," Pop Pop said, pointing to a pantry, "we have all the breads, crackers, and snacks atop my cutting board so I can easily grab them while I'm cooking. A proper chef always has all the tools within arm's reach."

Cole stood next to him, behind the narrow cutting board where he prepared all his food, which faced the window where people would soon begin to line up. "See, when I stand here, I can greet customers and always reach for everything I need without even thinking. People say, 'Chef Fantastico, I'd like a stack of pancakes, two slices of toast, and a bag of chips,' and Pop Pop knows exactly where everything is."

"Pop Pop, I bet Mommy would give you a sticker for being so organized. She gives me stickers when I put my pajamas in the hamper."

He laughed loudly. "You're right! It's good to be organized, and very professional, too."

Cole lifted his chin proudly. "I'm a professional chef."

"You can be one day, if you like. As I was saying, to my right are all the toppings, which I already have prepared. On this side, I have all my breads lined up neatly, all types along with dressings, too. This way, I have both hands working everything I need. And the fridge is right under me so, BOOM, I can get everything I need in an instant. You never want to make a customer wait."

Cole seemed fascinated by Pop Pop's process. I could tell just by listening to the way he oohhed and ahhed whenever Pop Pop described something. "Cole, if you want to be a great chef, you have to be fast and precise. People spend their hard-earned money and expect a great meal. It's Pop Pop's job to make sure they're happy and that they come back."

"Pop Pop, that is soooooo cool! But there's no way you can keep track of everything all the time. What happens when a bazillion people are yelling at you at the same time?"

Pop Pop laughed. "Well, we usually don't get a bazillion, but we do have dozens at a time, which is good for business. That's the life of a food truck. Luckily, Pop Pop has magic and that's what makes it work."

Again with that stupid magic stuff, I snorted, feeling irritated. I'm so tired of hearing about that fake magic. Where is it, huh? Where's that awe-inspiring magic you speak of?

"Like this, Cole," Pop Pop was saying. "Watch one example of Pop Pop's magic." He took a navy blue and white colored bandana out of his pocket and tied it around his head, covering his eyes. "I am completely blindfolded, right?"

Cole nodded, seeming curious and at the same time confused.

Pop Pop called out to my mom, "Sydney, do you agree that I'm one hundred percent, completely blindfolded?"

That means puppy in Italian. I watched him give Tucker a pancake.

"These pancakes are the most delicious thing I've ever had," I said.

"That makes my heart melt like butter in a hot pan," he replied. "You know what the best part is?"

"What's that?" I asked between bites.

"They aren't just pancakes, they're magical pancakes."

Ugh, again with the magic.

I rolled my eyes. "Look, Pop Pop, I know what you're trying to do here, but I'm not Cole. You don't have to do the whole magic thing with me. There's no such thing as magic pancakes or magic jackets, Pop Pop."

"There is too!"

I put my fork down. "Pop Pop, your food is amazing, but it's yours, not magic. You did it, not some fairy godmother with a magic wand."

Pop Pop rose from his chair and walked to the other side of the table, facing me. He stroked his mustache and looked up at the ceiling.

"Maddy, did I ever tell you how I got the name Fantastico?"

"I thought you just chose it because it sounded like a cool name to put on your food truck."

"True, it works nicely that way, but I didn't choose it myself."

"Then how?"

"I was given that nickname."

"By who?"

"Before Pop Pop was a chef, do you know what I did?" He put his hands on his hips.

"Kind of. You had a bunch of jobs, I think. Weren't you like a boxer or something? I've heard you talking about it before, but honestly, Pop Pop, I thought those were just stories you told Cole before he went to bed. Like the time you told me you had a pet cat who had rainbow colored fur. I mean, you're kinda funky like that sometimes, Pop Pop."

"Ah yes, sometimes Pop Pop goes for a good laugh, but not all my stories are pretend. See, I have been cooking my entire life, but before I became a chef and got my very own truck, I had to make money to get by. Before I met your grandma and before your Mommy was born, your Pop Pop was a world-famous professional wrestler."

I nearly choked on my pancakes. "Wait? What?"

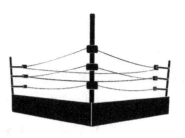

The High Flying Fantastico

I've heard a lot of whacky things, but Pop Pop telling me he was a professional wrestler topped everything. I couldn't believe all those stories Pop Pop told me and Cole about his wrestling days were real. I figured that was just another way of entertaining us, like the time he told me he ran a full marathon while balancing a banana on his forehead. I knew that story was ridiculous, but my Pop Pop as a wrestler? Now that's bananas. Or at least, I thought it was.

"Hold on, hold on. Time out." I made a 'T' with my hands. "You're telling me that you were like those wild, tough guys on TV, like the wrestlers Cole watches? The ones who fly all over the ring, wearing little tights and stuff, holding up gold belts when they win?"

"How dare you!" Pop Pop glared at me, and I felt a little scared until a smile broke across his face. "It was not wild; it was serious. And about those belts, I'll have you know I have one. The most important one, in fact. Your Pop Pop was a world champion, Maddy!"

"NO WAY!"

"It's the truth! People from all over would come to see me wrestle men who were two or three times my size. I'd come to the ring in the colors of the Italian flag with a long green cape, bright white wrestling trunks, and shiny red wrestling boots that ended right below my knees. Oh, Maddy, you should have seen it. When I put that cape on, it was as if I could do anything. I felt like a superhero. It was magical, Maddy. Simply magical."

I wagged my finger at him. "No way, Pop Pop. You're just pulling my leg. I mean, no offense or anything, but the wrestlers on TV are like gigantic. You're kind of short. Again, no offense."

"None taken. No matter how small you may be, you can always stand tall," Pop Pop said. "Yes, it's fair to say that Pop Pop Fantastico isn't a giant like you said, but what I lacked in height I made up for by being strong, gritty...and I could fly." He extended his arms and tilted his head as though he was soaring through the air. "Maddy Moo, I could fly through the air like an eagle. I'd climb to the top turnbuckle, then leap off the top rope with ease."

"Off the top rope?" I gasped.

"Yes! Very high. The higher, the better."

"That's why they called you Fantastico? Because you could jump so high?" I asked while I shoveled some fruit in my mouth.

"Not right away, Maddy. See, one day I was given the opportunity to fight this behemoth of a man named Hunter 'the Hammer' Harmon. He got his nickname because his hands were so thick and hard, they felt like actual hammers."

"Um, that doesn't sound like an opportunity so much as a death wish. It's like, 'Hey, Maddy, want to fight some guy they call the Hammer because his hands can literally squash people in a second?' I would be like, 'No, thanks. I'll pass and save myself the agony. Thanks, but no thanks.' That's what I'd say, Pop Pop."

"No, no, no, Maddy, in wrestling this was a very big opportunity. The Hammer was undefeated and the reigning world champion at the time. Even though the odds were not in my favor, I accepted right away. Before I went to the ring, my manager was begging me to disqualify myself. I didn't listen, though. I put my cape on, tightened my boots and ran to the ring when my name was announced. During the match, I tried my best, but Hunter was just too big for me. He weighed well over four hundred pounds and had a good foot and a half on me. In the middle of the match, I actually thought to myself, 'There is no way I can win.'"

"It took you until the middle of the match to realize that? I told you, Pop Pop, I would have known after I heard the whole 'fists like a hammer' thing."

"You can't back down without trying, Maddy."

"I'm not a fighter, Pop Pop, so maybe I missed something."

He lowered his voice, his tone stern, his eyes narrowing. "Not all fights involve fists, but everyone is a fighter. Most fights happen on the inside," he said, placing his hand on his heart. "The fight might make you ask yourself, 'What is worth standing up for? What do you really want?' For me, it was the world title."

"So, Pop Pop, did you lose?" I asked, folding my arms on the table.

He acted out the match as he talked, making increasingly exaggerated movements with every word. He pressed his hands against his lower back, as if he was still in pain from the match. "Wait, wait, wait, Maddy. Right as Hunter was getting ready to set me up for his big finisher that would surely knock me down, while my entire body was aching, I heard the crowd start to chant my name over and over and over." He pumped his fists to mimic the fans cheering him on to get up and fight back. "All that cheering infuriated Hunter, but it gave me energy. It gave me strength to push on." As if his arms were pistons, Pop Pop started punching the air.

"The fans were on your side?"

Pop Pop scooted around the kitchen floor. "Oh, they were, Maddy!" He lifted his hands over his head, as if pushing a heavy rock off his shoulders. "When Hunter picked me up for a big body slam, I got away." Then he crawled on the floor to demonstrate. "Hunter tried to catch me again, but I jumped up and kicked him in the stomach. He started to buckle, so I did it again and again."

As if he was one of the fans, Tucker ran around Pop Pop's feet, getting caught up in the excitement.

"That's right, Pop Pop! You have to stand up to bullies," I shouted, bouncing in my seat.

Pop Pop got to his feet, then grabbed his stomach. "As Hunter bent over in pain, holding his stomach and letting out a monstrous roar, I seized the moment."

My eyes were so wide, I thought they might pop off my face like Pop Pop from the top rope. "What did you do?"

Pop Pop bounced like a cat, onto the kitchen chair. "As he moaned in pain, I rolled him up like a ball of dough, holding his neck with my left arm, and one of his legs with my right arm. I clasped my hands together as tight as possible so he couldn't escape. He was so big, and my arms could not hold him for long, so I had to dig as deep as I could to keep his shoulders on the mat. I held on as if my life depended on it," he said, wrapping his arms across his chest as if trying to hug his own back.

"And then what happened, Pop Pop? What happened?"

"Seeing that I had him for the pin, even the referee couldn't believe it, the crowd couldn't believe it, and of course Hunter couldn't believe it. But the referee dropped to the mat, and then, just as the Hammer was trying to fight and wiggle his way out, the entire crowd counted in unison with the referee as his hand slapped the canvas. They shouted, one, and Hunter tried to escape, so I held him down even harder. Then two, and again he started to buck his way out, yet it was too late.

The referee counted to three, and I had pinned the great Hunter 'the Hammer' Harmon, right there in the middle of the ring—one, two, and three! Your Pop Pop was the new Heavyweight Champion of the World!"

As he breathed heavily from all the energy he poured into the story, he took a hand towel and held it over his head as if he'd been holding a belt. "I took that world title belt and danced around the ring for twenty minutes. As I celebrated my win, everyone started talking about how fantastic it was. Knowing I was Italian, the crowd started chanting, Fantastico, Fantastico, Fantastico! From that day on, until the day I retired from the ring, I was known around the world as Fantastico the Magnificent!"

I clapped. "Bravo, bravo, bravo to the great Fantastico! Wow, I had no idea. You're like a superhero, Pop Pop."

"No, not a superhero at all. I simply saw something I wanted, and I went after it. I didn't listen to the doubters who told me I had no chance. I followed my heart, and that's what I've done every day since with my food."

I shook my head in amazement.

"Don't you strive for something?" Pop Pop asked.

I thought for a second. "Well, there is something I've really had my eye on."

"Okay, what is it?"

My cheeks turned red. "It's nothing. I mean, it's not becoming champion of the world or anything super cool like what you did."

Pop Pop placed a gentle hand on my shoulder. He looked me straight in the eye and said, "Maddy, always remember, anything you want in life that is worth chasing after is never nothing."

"Even a new bike?"

"Ah, yes, a new bike. Your mom mentioned that to me."

"See, I told you it wasn't that big of a deal. I mean, I want it really, really, super, crazy bad, but I can't afford it, and it's really expensive."

Pop Pop scratched his mustache. "Hmm, I wonder if there is a way to get you that bike, so you could earn it?"

"Yeah," I said, curious about what he had in mind.

"Ah, I got it! Pop Pop has an idea."

"You do? Really? What is it?"

He pulled out a folded piece of paper. "Have you heard about this food truck competition that I'm going to be in? The Grand Prix I believe it's called. There's a very big prize."

World Champion Food Truck Chefs

After realizing Pop Pop's idea was to win the Grand Prix, my excitement level sank into my stomach like a pile of rocks. Based on the competition from the other night, I didn't think we had a chance to win fortieth place, let alone first.

"I don't know, Pop Pop. I am not sure that plan will work."

He arched his neck. "What do you mean?"

"The thing is, it's like the best trucks in town. As much as everyone loves your food, the other trucks..." Realizing my next words may hurt his feelings, I stopped. "Never mind, Pop Pop."

He smiled knowingly. "Maddy, my love, I think I know what you are trying to say."

"You do?"

"You think Pop Pop's food truck is not as impressive as the others, correct?"

I felt miserable for even thinking it and sad for having to hear Pop Pop say it out loud. I felt like I might cry. "I'm so sorry, Pop Pop. I didn't mean to hurt your feelings."

Then he cupped my cheeks in his hands and kissed my forehead. "Maddy, dear, you could never ever hurt my feelings."

"Really?"

"Yes, really," he said, smiling. "Plus, it's okay. I know my truck is not so up-to-date or as sleek as the others. You're not pointing out anything new. But remember my story about how I defeated the Hammer?"

"Yeah, but what does wrestling have to do with operating a food truck or being a chef?" I asked, confused.

"Everything! There I was, the underdog, the unlikely one, the one no one thought could win...

and I did it. I beat him! I beat him with my heart and my desire to be extraordinary. That's how we're going to win the contest, and that's how we're going to get you a new bike."

"I've never really thought of myself as extraordinary though, Pop Pop."

Pop Pop cupped my face in his hands. "I'd rather live every day trying to be extraordinary and fail, than settle for the safety of being ordinary and never know what I could become."

He was right. We had to try. We had to take the risk. "Really? You'd do that for me?"

"I'll do it for us." Pop Pop smiled so bright his mouth could stretch a mile. "Anything for my family, anything at all. To win, though, I'll need both you and Cole to help me out, along with Mom, Dad, and maybe your friend Ella, if she's interested. You will work for me and earn that money for the bike and together we will be World Champion Food Truck Chefs!"

"You got it!" I got up and hugged him tightly. "Oh, Pop Pop, I love you!"

"Tomorrow after school, I'll have Mommy drop you off at my truck, and then we can get started with your training. This won't be easy, Maddy. It will be a challenge, but we can do it together." He stretched his hands in the air. "We will be victorious."

"Victory!" I shouted.

He grabbed my hand, and we started dancing around the kitchen. We skipped, hand in hand, chanting, "We will win! We will win! We will win!"

We were cheering so loud that we didn't hear Ella walk into the kitchen. "Nice of you to let me in on the first knock. It took five times before your mom finally opened the door."

"Sorry, Ella, we were a little busy," I said, laughing while I skipped around with Pop Pop.

"What are you two doing?"

Pop Pop grabbed Ella's hand, pulling her away from the doorway to the kitchen. "Come dance! Come celebrate with us!"

Ella laughed and shouted along in unison.

"We're going to win the Grand Prix, Ella!"

She threw her hands in the air. "I told you that you could do it, Maddy!"

That'll Be The Day

After we devoured a breakfast fit for a queen of the court, we were off to school. During the ride, Ella and I discussed the plans for the food truck and how incredible our win would be. My mom glanced at us through the mirror every time we high-fived, which was a lot.

"It sounds like you're up to something interesting back there," she said.

"Oh it's nothing, Mom. We're simply planning on dominating the world of food trucks. That's all." We high-fived again.

After being dropped off, we walked into school like rock stars. My confidence was so high, I could practically feel the electricity running through my body. I felt like I was standing in front of a stadium of people, and they were chanting my name. "Maddy! Maddy! Maddy! We love you, Maddy! You're the best chef in the world! Hey, Maddy, what kind of bike did you get?"

Oh, man, this is going to be awesome-sauce, I thought.

The Grand Prix was within my grasp, and it was only a matter of time before I would be able to ride my new bike to school and gloat to all my friends...especially that mean, nasty, rude, obnoxious classmate of mine, Kenny. I held my head high as I strutted around the halls in my green t-shirt with Pop Pop's logo on it, making sure everyone knew I was proud to represent his truck. As I made my way into homeroom, Kenny swaggered by, wearing a shirt that advertised his father's food truck. It was bright green and it read *Zalis Burgers!* in neon yellow.

"Maddy, what's with the shirt?" Kenny asked, sneering at me.

"This is my Pop Pop's food truck, Fanastico's Fantastic Food Truck. You may have heard of it. It's practically legendary," I said proudly. Then I leaned in close, waving my index finger in the air. "And guess what? We are going to win the Grand Prix!"

Kenny backed up in shock, as if I'd scared him. It turned out he was faking. His pal, Walter, laughed loudly and slapped Kenny's back. "Do you hear that? Maddy thinks her grandfather's beat-up ole rust wagon is going to win. Dude, is that the funniest thing you've ever heard, or what?"

Kenny laughed and slapped his knee. "I think you must have been standing too close to the microwave, Maddy, because it must have zapped your brain. That's crazy talk!"

I put my hands on my hips and stood my ground. "Go ahead and laugh now, but I'll have the last laugh this weekend."

My comeback didn't resonate with Kenny. He and Walter cackled uncontrollably, then fell to the ground and laughed with their hands on their stomachs. They could hardly breathe from laughing so hard.

"This is the wildest thing I've ever heard!" Kenny shouted. "Girls as chefs? Girls can't be chefs!"

"A girl and some old man in a ragged truck winning the Grand Prix?" Walter added. "That'll be the day. Hope you brought some more shirts with you, Maddy, because Kenny will use them to mop the floor after his dad's food truck wins."

Before I could say anything, other kids had gathered around. They laughed along with Kenny and Walter. Some of them pointed at me and whispered to each other. I wasn't even sure they knew what they were laughing about, but they were encouraging these two bullies. No one should have to tolerate that.

I felt like my feet were trapped in ice. I couldn't move.

Ella rushed to my aid. "Don't let them get to you, Maddy. Come on. They'll see how great your Pop Pop's food truck can be."

At the start of the day, I'd felt so confident, but now Kenny, Walter, and my classmates had me doubting myself—and Pop Pop, for that matter. We walked off in silence, leaving the other kids laughing behind us.

No Being Sad Rule

All day long, I couldn't shake the voices in my head reminding me of the other kids laughing at me. But why did I let it bother me? I know what our truck can do, and I don't care what mean people say. Still, why did it get to me? Were they right? Was I wrong? Throughout the day, Ella looked at me every so often and gave me a thumbs up to try to make me feel better, but it didn't help. As usual, Mom met me in the school's carpool and pick-up area at the end of the day with Cole tucked in his car seat. I slid into the car, then rolled down the seat into a tiny ball and pulled my hooded sweatshirt as far over my face as I could. Mom could tell I was upset again.

"Sweetheart, did something happen at school?"

I shook my head.

"Did everyone like your shirt?"

Again, I shook my head.

"Do you want to talk about it?"

For a third time, I shook my head.

Cole thought he could comfort me. He sweetly reached out his tiny hand to grab mine. I gently squeezed his fingers in return so he would know I appreciated the gesture.

"Maddy, we all have bad days, even buccaneers like me and Buster. Remember what Pop Pop always says: Keep your head up, and never give up. Remember that? I think you should do that." Then he tilted his chin upward and smiled. "See, watch me. Look at my head. It's held high."

From the rearview mirror, my mom smiled at Cole.

He wasn't finished lending his opinions. "Plus, there's the 'No Being Sad Rule' on Pop Pop's food truck."

"Wait, what did you say?" I asked.

"I said, there's the 'No Being Sad Rule' on Pop Pop's food truck."

"The food what?"

"Food truck!" he shouted. "Geez Louise, you need to clean out your ears, Maddy Moo."

I sat up. "Coley! You didn't mix up your letters."

"What?"

"Say food truck."

"Food truck," he replied.

"Hear that? You didn't say twuck, you said truck with an R sound," I exclaimed, cheering for him.

"I did! I did! Look at that."

"I'm very proud of you, Cole," Mom said.

"And I am, too, little buddy," I added.

Whether it was Cole's sweet touch, or finally working out the letters that he'd struggled with for so long, something got me out of my food truck funk. I don't know how to explain it, but hearing Cole—a little-bitty kid—repeat what Pop Pop had preached to us so often, and in the proper way, just lifted me out of my grogginess. I pulled back my hood and sat up straight in my seat.

"You're right, Cole," I said.

"I am right? Me? Cole is right?" he asked, seeming surprised.

"Yup, you. My little buccaneer of a brother is totally, absolutely, positively correct."

"Mommy, did you hear that? I'm right. I cheered up Maddy."

"You did more than just cheer me up, little buddy."

I rolled down my window and let the air blow against my face. I leaned my head out, which made my mother very scared.

"Madilyn Avery! Please put your head back into the car!" she hollered.

"One second, Mom," I said over the sound of the rushing wind. "I just have to tell the world one thing." I took a deep breath and with every bit of strength my lungs could spare, I shouted, "Hey, world, you'd better be ready, because Pop Pop, Cole and I are going to be the greatest chefs you've ever seen!"

***

Training for the Grand Prix started that night and continued for two hours every night. It was like a culinary boot camp. After learning the ropes from Pop Pop, I had to get home, do homework, and get to bed. Even though I had responsibilities for school, I didn't worry about them while I was with Pop Pop. During our time, I was solely dedicated to learning everything I could about becoming a chef. After school, we'd go wherever Pop Pop parked his truck, and I'd assist in any way I could. I watched everything Pop Pop did, from how he greeted customers with a smile and a cheery voice, to how he took their orders.

"Maddy, we have to move fast," he said, flipping the page over in his tiny pocket notebook. "I don't bother writing the entire order word for word. I shorten them." Then he showed me his scribble.

I squinted at the order. "Pop Pop, that doesn't make any sense. You wrote, *1 tk, san, w/ l, t, m on rb,*. That looks like gibberish."

He read it out loud from memory as he made the sandwich. "One turkey sandwich, with lettuce, tomato, and mayonnaise on rye bread. I just shortened it. You have to move fast! Get it right, and make it look magnificent, but always be on your toes."

I looked at it again. "Oh. Well, that does make sense, I guess."

There is a lot about being a chef I'll have to learn.

"Anyone can stack lettuce on top of bread and wipe some mayonnaise on it. I look at making food like making a masterpiece. I look at each item as a part of my life, which I'm sharing with a customer, and I do not want to disappoint them." Pop Pop opened the bin of vegetables he used for sandwiches. "These bright green pickles here, or these deliciously red tomatoes right here, and these luscious blueberries, they are all far more than just fruits and vegetables. They come from all over the country, from different people in different walks of life." He then took my left hand and placed a bunch of blueberries in my palm.

"All the colors, all the textures in the foods come together like the madras pattern of my pants. That's why I love them so much. I, just like our heritage, am a pattern."

"These blueberries are so rich, they look more like jewels from a buried treasure than fruit for a salad."

Pop Pop grabbed one and placed it into his mouth. "All of this food is a part of me, a part of my work, and a part of our culture."

I ate the remaining four blueberries. "Mmmmm!"

"It's like our chef pants, you see? All these wonderful patterns coming together to make something beautiful. In the same way, my heart is filled with all the wondrous colors found on my pants and in my food and in the food of all the cultures throughout the world."

It was incredible to listen to Pop Pop talk about his love for cooking. I had never thought about food that way, or even imagined the colors in our chef pants could have a bigger meaning. Each day was a new lesson, from another part of the menu to the operating side of running a truck. One night we even went to a local produce market to buy farm fresh ingredients from farmers around the area. He walked around like the president—shaking hands, saying hello to everyone, and making small talk as we shopped. My favorite moment was when we bought ten pounds of homemade chocolate chips from a baker who came to America from Paris. Pop Pop has known him for years, and they have been friends since he was in his twenties—which is a super-long time.

The next day we used those same chocolate chips in several pancake orders, which was a tasty lesson. Turns out people like pancakes in the evening, too!

"Come watch the pancakes dance, Maddy."

"Dancing pancakes, Pop Pop?"

"You'll see," he said.

He took me by the hand, and we bent down to look closer at the pan, as Pop Pop slowly poured the thick batter out of a ladle, forming three softball sized pancakes. The pan came to life as the batter met the melted butter and began to sizzle on contact.

He spoke in a hushed tone, as if he'd wake up the pancake had he spoken any louder. "Watch, Maddy.... Watch..."

I looked at Pop Pop, who kept his stare locked on the hot pan. And then, just as he said, the pancake started to, well...dance. The sides began to bubble and turn a dark gold color.

"Now, we flip!" Pop Pop said, standing up and flipping a pancake with a spatula.

In less than a second, the pancake was cooking on the other side.

"Your turn," he said.

"Oh, I don't know, Pop Pop."

"You can do it. Here, take the spatula," he said, placing my hand on the wooden handle and his over top of mine. "And one, two, flip!"

"We did it," I said.

"This one on your own, now," he said, backing away.

"I can't, Pop Pop."

"You can, and you must! Look, it will get too brown. Only a second left."

I took a deep breath and then shimmied the metal head of the spatula under the pancake and flipped it as fast as I could.

"*Perfecto!*" Pop Pop said, clapping, admiring my perfectly cooked pancake.

It was amazing to watch Pop Pop put such care into every part of the cooking process. Everything he did had a purpose, and he never stopped smiling, no matter how busy we got. Although, whether it was making pancakes, sandwiches, or taking orders, not everything was so glamorous. One time he made me clean out the ovens with a sponge, and I had to wash dishes. Ugh, some things about being a chef were nasty, but I didn't care; I was a working chef on a real food truck.

After every shift Pop Pop and I took a half hour to powwow with one another about the Grand Prix—ideas for food, roles for everyone, what we had in inventory and what we needed to buy. I kept a journal of everything I did and what I learned. I wanted to remember what happened each day to think about how I could have made it better. I fell asleep with my journal on my stomach every night as if it was one of my stuffed animals. It was the last thing I saw before bed and the first thing I woke up to. Training for the Grand Prix wasn't easy, but it was invigorating. Magic or no magic, if this was what it felt like to be a chef, I could do this for the rest of my life.

The Night Before the Grand Prix

While organizing my stuffed animals for bedtime later that night—two teddy bears, one stuffed smiley emoji, and a big fluffy pink letter M—my Dad walked into my bedroom with his phone in his hand. "Sweetie, it's Pop Pop. He wants to video chat with you."

I grabbed the phone as if it was on fire and only my hands could put it out. I was so thrilled to talk to Pop Pop that I didn't even make eye contact with him at first; I started rambling a mile a minute. I twirled around with the phone like a ballerina, leaping from each side of the room, full of energy.

"Hey, Pop Pop! It's almost the big day, and I can't wait. We have so much to go over, but it's okay, because I. Am. Pumped! Pumped, I tell you. PUUUUUUMPED!"

"Maddy, I need to talk to you," Pop Pop said softly.

"I'm also on chapter four of a marketing book I got from the library," I continued, barely hearing his interruptions. "This chapter talks about making yourself into a brand, which you've done very well so far, and how to make people identify you in a crowd of competitors. Perfect for our current situation. I have a great idea, too. I've been working on it since dinner."

"Maddy—"

"First we'll lay out the breads and then work on prepping the meats. You can start cutting, and I'll work on the toppings."

"Maddy, wait—"

"I know, I know, I can't touch the knives. Knives are for grown-ups and experienced chefs only, blah, blah-blah, blah-blah."

"That is correct, but that's not why I called. I have to talk to you about something, and it's very important."

"Well, what is it, silly? You have me so excited that I'm just blabbing away over here."

"This," Pop Pop said, and then pointed toward his left leg, showing a cast covering his entire foot and ending right under his knee.

"What happened?" I gasped.

Pop Pop shook his head. "Earlier today, I was carrying a box of potatoes when I slipped on the steps and felt a sharp pain shoot through my leg. I went to the emergency room, and the doctor said I broke my leg."

Tears filled my eyes. "But Pop Pop, does this mean..."

"I know what you're thinking. The Grand Prix, right?"

"Does this mean we can't go?"

Pop Pop didn't answer right away, and as I stared at him, tears running off my chin, he started to smile.

"What are you smiling about, Pop Pop?" I asked.

"Everything."

"Everything? What do you mean?"

I flopped down on my bed, my arms spread, the phone clutched in my hand as I stared at the ceiling fan spinning around, just like the emotions in my head.

I went down the list of reasons my life was crumbling in front of me. "We have nothing now," I said. "You're hurt, and we have to cancel our entry in the Grand Prix. I'll never get the money for the bike, and all my friends will laugh at me, especially that mean ol' Kenny, and his goober friend, Walter. Oh, Pop Pop, my life will be over! Wait, did I mention all my friends will laugh at me? If I did, I feel that needs to be mentioned again."

"Maddy, can you please look at the phone? I'm staring at your ceiling fan and getting rather dizzy," Pop Pop said.

"Yeah, well, welcome to my world, Pop Pop. I feel like my life is spinning out of control."

His laughter came through the speaker. I didn't know what was funny, and his reaction annoyed me. I turned the phone to face him.

"How can you laugh at a time like this? Huh? What is so funny? Why are you not upset?"

He shook his head and grinned. "You don't get it, Maddy."

"Oh, I get it all right. You? Not so much. Here, I'll explain it. Your leg is broken. Which, by the way, I feel terrible about—"

"It's okay. I'll heal."

"When you fell, you must have hit your head, because clearly you don't get it. I may have to talk to Mommy and Daddy about your sanity."

Pop Pop nearly wept with laughter. "Oh, Maddy, you crack me up."

"I still don't get it. Why aren't you as upset as I am?"

Pop Pop finally calmed down as he wiped tears of laughter from his eyes. "Maddy, look at me. I may have a broken leg, but we are still going to enter, and more importantly, we are still going to win!"

"How?"

"You like playing basketball, right?" he asked.

"Of course, but I'm not making it into the WNBA any time soon, Pop Pop. Come on, get with the program. Work with me here. Work. With. Me!"

"Oh, gosh, Maddy...you are too, too much. In basketball, you have a coach. The coach isn't on the court shooting baskets, right?"

"No, he's not."

"He's on the sideline giving you advice. I will be the coach. I will be in the truck helping you out. I'll be on a stool and standing, when I can. Your dad will be there to help and can guide that traffic, too. He's worked many times in my truck under even more challenging predicaments. Just like on the court, we'll work as a team. After all, I can still use my arms, hands, and my other leg. One broken leg is not the end of the world, let alone the end of our chances of winning the Grand Prix."

I nodded. "Ohhhhh, now I get it. Okay, phew," I said. "I thought for a second you were going to tell me you weren't able to cook at all."

"Well, actually, that's why we'll need Cole to help out."

"Cole? If I can't touch knives or hot items, how can he? He can't do anything. He's practically a baby. A baby who thinks he's a pirate. I once asked him to pick out a piece of fruit he wanted for a snack, and he told me he wanted popcorn. We had a thirty-minute debate about how popcorn is not a fruit or a vegetable. Is that the kind of cuckoo clock you want runnin' things in your truck, Pop Pop?"

"Dear, the food truck is a family truck and together, as a family, we will work as a team. But I don't think we'll let Cole take orders. I mean, they can't order Pop Pop's famous Indulgent Chocolate Chip Pancake Special and end up with a tomato sandwich instead, right?"

"Yup, Cole would totally do that."

"Don't worry, we'll find something for him to do. Big or small, old or young, a family business is about family first."

"What now, Pop Pop?"

"Maddy, I've been down before but never out, and I've always come back to win. Remember how I defeated the Hammer? I will win again. We will—me, you, Cole, Mom, Dad. Together, as a family, we will win the Grand Prix! But I'm definitely going to need your help to make it happen."

"Pop Pop, say no more. You are in good hands."

"I have no doubt, *il mio amore*."

I knew that was Italian for 'my love'.

"Now, get some rest. Tomorrow morning before the sun comes up, Mommy and Daddy will drop you both off and we'll get to work. Remember Maddy, Pop Pop Fantastico never backs down from a challenge, and tomorrow, no matter how big or fancy the other trucks are, we will show them how extraordinary we can be."

I liked the sound of that. I rose to my feet and stuck my thumb up in front of the camera. "You got it, Pop Pop. Tomorrow, we'll be kings."

"In our hearts, we're already kings!"

"Yeah, kings with fancy new bikes!" I shouted, jumping up and down on my bed.

The Big, Huge, Mega-Important Day: The Grand Prix

As much as I didn't like getting up for school super early, I was ready and willing to beat the sunrise on the day of the Grand Prix. I didn't sleep very much at all. How could I? From reading my marketing book to developing the finishing touches on my new addition to Pop Pop's truck (to help drive revenue, which is a business word that basically means the money you bring into your company) sleeping was the last thing on my mind. However, when I finally got into bed, I still tossed and turned. I counted the glow in the dark stickers of the solar system I had stuck to the ceiling over my bed. Usually, when I couldn't sleep, I counted to around thirty—but not last night. I counted all one hundred and forty-five of them, plus all the planets, the moon, and a freaky little neon alien family in the corner of the ceiling. None of it helped me sleep. Yeesh, that was a lot of counting.

I remembered what Pop Pop said about his big match against the Hammer, and how he couldn't sleep either. He said it was because of adrenaline pumping through his veins. Apparently, adrenaline is something in your body that makes you like crazy-excited and anxious all at the same time. If that's true, then my cup is running over with adrenaline. Maybe that's why I wasn't even tired. Thanks, adrenaline! We're going to get along famously.

I don't remember if I actually slept, but pretty soon the sun was coming up and I was deep into the process of getting dressed. I had my madras pants and chef's coat ironed and looking sharp.

My shoelaces were tied tight so I wouldn't trip (every chef has to be careful in the kitchen), and I'd even buffed the rubber soles clean for an extra bit of professionalism. I heard my dad knock on my bedroom door just as I was positioning my handkerchief in the chest pocket of my jacket the same way Pop Pop does every day.

Dad knocked gently again, as if assuming I was still asleep. "Maddy Moo, it's time to get up," he whispered, so as not to wake Cole.

"You can come in, Dad. I'm ready to go."

"Wow!" he said, opening the door and surveying my outfit. "It's 5:45. I thought I'd have to drag you out of here."

"Nope. You guessed wrong, Dad. I'm all set. So, why don't you get dressed and run a comb through that bird's nest you call hair? Sound like a plan? We have work to do." I clapped my hands. "Chop, chop, Dad. That trophy is waiting for us."

"I like the energy, Moo. Can we get this on a regular basis?"

"Eh, don't count on it," I said, patting him on the back as I walked past him into the hallway.

"You have twenty-five minutes, old man, and we are out the door. I suggest you change into the family food truck uniform right away. I laid it out on your bed for both you and Mommy. Cole's outfit is in his room. I'll be waiting downstairs for you slackers."

"I thought that was Mommy. But I like that you're taking the initiative. Maybe you could do that for school as well."

"Again, don't get your hopes up. I'll be downstairs drinking my protein shake."

"Wait, since when do you drink protein shakes?"

"Gotta keep that energy going, Dad. Gotta put some hustle in the muscles," I said, hurrying down the steps.

I sat at the kitchen table sipping my banana-strawberry protein smoothie while going over my plans for the day. I meant business, and my face showed it. It's our time, and no one could take that away from us.

The Soon-To-Be Famous Maddy and Cole Cookie Company

"Drive faster, Daddy, let's go!" I shouted from the back seat.

"Honey, I'm going as fast as I can. Any faster and I'll get a speeding ticket. Trust me, even worse than being late would be having to explain to a police officer what's going on while we're all wearing matching uniforms at six in the morning. He'll think we're some kind of culinary bandits or something."

"I know, I know. I just can't wait to get there and dive into work. Pop Pop's been doing the prep work, but with only one leg, he can only do so much. He needs me. He needs my help!"

"Of course he does, Maddy, and we'll be there in a second," Mom said. "But keep your voice down. Cole is still sleeping."

Yup, he sure was. While I felt like I might jump out of my skin, my so-called assistant (stinky, smelly, sleepy Cole) was snoring away like a bear in hibernation.

"You mean this lil' slug? Puh-lease. Pop Pop said that real chefs wake up energized. Cole woke up, went back to sleep in the car, and when he wakes up again he'll probably ask for a snack and then want to go back to bed."

"Oh, sweetie, he'll be fine. Remember, the food truck is a family operation, and the whole family helps out."

I rolled my eyes. "Yeah, well, we'll see. Right now, I have to get my cookin' on, Momma."

***

When we arrived at Mt. Cedarmere Park, the scene was even crazier than I imagined. Trucks from all over were gathered in a large circle, leaving only enough room to walk between each one to carry supplies and keep the flow of foot traffic moving. In the middle was a grand stage, adorned with green and white balloons (those are the Mt. Cedarmere colors) with a gold trophy and a microphone stand. On that stage, they would announce the winner. Man, oh, man—it was an amazing sight. Dozens and dozens of food trucks were everywhere. They were decked out to the nines, wearing their best and shiniest coats of wax, and wheels gleaming.

There were picnic tables in front of the trucks where customers could dine. Most trucks had gimmicks to draw more attention, like a juggler or a magician. One truck even had one of those dancing inflatable neon aliens hooked up to a fan. When the fan was on full speed, the alien stood up about ten feet tall and swayed in the wind. Now that was pretty neat!

It turned out that everyone else got the memo about helping each food truck. Every truck had its own team, all wearing matching uniforms. Even on the busiest of days, a truck like Howard and

Robin's New York Pizza only has three workers max, but today it had eight! This didn't bother me too much. The only thing it meant was that everyone was here for business. No goofing around, no playing nice. This is war!

Pop Pop was inside the truck when my mom honked the car horn to get his attention. He popped his head out of the ordering station window wearing his chef's hat and a big smile on his face.

"*La mia famiglia!*" he shouted. That meant 'my family' in Italian.

"*Ciao Nonno!*" I replied, meaning, 'Hello, Grandfather'. There's no official Italian word for Pop Pop.

"Ah, Maddy, you've been practicing your Italian, I see," he said happily.

"That's right, Dad," Mom said, "she's embracing her heritage."

Pop Pop blew kisses to us with his hands. "Oh dear, a Pop Pop can only be so lucky to have that kind of support. Now, come, come," he said, waving his hands. "We have to get ready before the opening ceremonies. Wait right there. I'm coming out."

While Pop Pop came out to meet us, my dad handed me a wicker picnic basket with something special for Pop Pop. I had spent all night working on it.

"Go ahead, sweetie. Show it to Pop Pop."

I winked at my dad as he placed the basket next to me so I could give Pop Pop a hug.

"Easy does it, guys. Don't forget about Pop Pop's leg," Mom said.

Cole and I ran into the truck to greet Pop Pop with hugs, while my mom and dad carried supplies. Pop Pop hobbled down the two steps leading into the truck to meet us, and I finally got a chance to see his injured leg in person.

He wobbled out of the truck, a wooden cane by his side.

"Yikes, Pop Pop! You look like a robot." Cole gasped.

Pop Pop laughed and tapped his soft brace with the cane. "I think a robot wouldn't need a cane, though."

"Pop Pop, that doesn't look so good," I said, concerned. "Are you sure you'll be okay to move around today?"

"Don't worry, Maddy," Mom said. "I once saw Pop Pop change a spare tire with a broken collar bone. This is nothing."

"Is that true, Pop Pop?"

"It is. And just as I did then, I did not think about the pain. Remember my battle with the Hammer? I didn't care about pain then, and it was way worse. I surely won't worry about it now. You'll just have to help me reach for things. Other than that, it's just another day at the office."

Makes sense to me, I thought.

Pop Pop bent at his waist, since he couldn't bend from his legs, and held my hands with Cole's. "Wait a second, my loves. Look at your jackets!" Pop Pop said rubbing his fingers over Cole's buttons. He noticed that I replaced them with odd-matching buttons just like his.

"I made some alterations," I said.

"I love it!" he said standing back up and opening his hands wide.

"Do you see this, Sydney? Do you see what your daughter did?"

"What can I say, she learned from the best." Mom and Dad opened their winter coats to reveal their newly placed buttons on their chef jackets as well.

Pop Pop looked up at the sky. "*La mia famiglia!*" he said laughing.

He bent back down to grab our hands in his again. "Today is a big day, my loves. Right?" Then he kissed our hands.

"Big day. Huge day!" Cole said.

"That's right, Pop Pop, it's a big day, and we're going to crush the competition."

"We'll see about that." Pop Pop chuckled. "Let's focus on making the best food we can for our customers."

"Come on, Pop Pop, you have to appreciate Maddy's competitiveness," Dad said.

"It is rather refreshing." Pop Pop blushed. Then he looked down at my basket. "Maddy, what's in there?"

Dad nodded. "Go ahead," he said. "Show Pop Pop what you brought."

I opened the lid, revealing my own personal addition to Pop Pop's food truck.

"I call them *Maddy and Cole Cookies*." I handed him one. "You've inspired my entrepreneurial spirit. I can see the "Maddy and Cole Cookie Company" opening a shop one day. They're my own little take on a traditional chocolate-fudge topped sugar cookie. They're the same size as a regular chocolate chip cookie, with a nice, thick glob of fudge icing on top which complements the color of the cookie. I have purple-on-purple, chocolate-on-chocolate, and white-on-white for now. All chocolatey deliciousness, of course. I figure I can expand the line if it goes well. Expanding your brand was in my book, too."

Pop Pop picked up a purple-on-purple cookie, and a white-on-white one. He took a bite of each. Then he stepped back slowly. He didn't smile or say a word.

"You don't like them?" I asked.

He shook his head. "Just the opposite."

"Then why are you walking backward like that? I thought you were trying to get away from my cookies."

He stopped and smiled wide. "I'm not backing away because they're bad, I'm backing up, because I am losing my balance over how good they are! I've never tasted or seen anything like *Maddy and Cole Cookies* before. That buttery, delicious taste topped with luscious chocolate-fudge topping. Not to mention the variety of beautiful colors. Maddy Moo, these are...I can't find the word, they're..."

"Fantastic!" Cole shouted.

"Yes!" Pop Pop sang. "Yes, my dearest, they sure are fantastic. And today, they're going to be famous. We'll sell them at the counter where everyone will see them. They will want two, I promise you that! It's impossible to have only one."

"Geez, that marketing book really worked," I said.

The Madras Heart

After finishing four of my Maddy and Cole cookies, Pop Pop threw his hands in the air. "I was so happy to see you, I forgot to mention how amazing everyone looks today in your uniforms," Pop Pop said, practically glowing. "My darling daughter, your jacket and pants still fit the same way they did when you were in college. Reed, my son, we may have to take yours out a little bit!"

"Keep the jokes coming Pop Pop. Maybe if you stopped using me as your taste tester, I could hit the gym more often."

"Well, no one looks as good as my little ones right here," he said to me and Cole.

"Maddy, why don't you show Pop Pop what you added while Cole and I go set up," Mom said as she walked by with a box of paper plates. Cole followed behind her.

"What addition?" Pop Pop asked.

I unbuttoned my chef's coat, showing the company t-shirt, but on the inside of the left side of my coat was a three-inch heart patch made out of madras fabric, with a thin denim outline that Dad had sewn on the night before.

Pop Pop covered his mouth. "It's beautiful, Maddy."

"When my mom hemmed my pants to fit me properly, there was some left over material and it gave me an idea. You know how I love hearts, right?"

Pop Pop nodded.

"Well, all hearts are usually red or pink but when I look at a heart I don't see it as only one color; I see it as many colors, like the madras fabric. All sorts of colors, crossing back and forth, intertwining and mixing together to form a lovely image. It's like a family. Every family is different, and everyone brings their own uniqueness to the table. No matter where you go, no matter who you meet, I think it's better to remember how colorful life is."

Pop Pop kept his hand on his mouth, and I saw a small tear roll down his face.

"Oh, Pop Pop, did I upset you?"

He shook his head.

"But you're crying."

"You are full of surprises today, Maddy. I'm crying tears of joy, *il mio amore*," he said, still choked up. "This just proves how amazing your heart is, *nipotina*."

"I'm glad you like it, Pop Pop, because I made you one, too."

I reached into my back pocket and pulled out the same one for him. "I made everyone a heart. This way we all have something special to remind us of our family whenever we put on our uniforms."

Pop Pop reached down and lifted me up with one arm, as if he had no pain in his body at all.

"Pop Pop, you're going to hurt yourself again!"

"No, Maddy. Nothing can hurt me now! Come on, let's go sew this on my jacket right away. I have a sewing kit in the truck. I will never forget this gesture."

We sat in the front seats of Pop Pop's truck as he carefully sewed his madras heart patch onto his jacket, over the pocket. As we pulled the final strand through and tied it tight, we heard a voice over the loud speaker.

"Will all food truck team members please report to the stage for opening statements from Mayor Douglass."

"Ah, my loves, let's go, let's go! We can't keep the mayor waiting."

As we climbed out of the truck, crowds of people headed toward the stage. Pop Pop moved very well, despite his injury, hobbling along with only a slight limp thanks to his cane. Maybe that was part of the whole magic thing he kept talking about—his ability to block out the pain and continue to fight. Whatever it was, I dug it. I held Pop Pop's free hand, and Cole put his hand on Pop Pop's lower back.

"Don't worry, Pop Pop. If you fall, I'll catch you."

"Thanks for having my back, Coley," Pop Pop said.

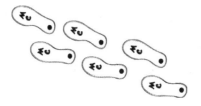

And Here We Go

Mayor Douglass has been a figurehead in the city for over a decade. Her legacy in the town goes back more than half a century. Her grandfather was the first African-American mayor of Mt. Cedarmere. After him, her father became the mayor and for the past three years, she has served as the first female, African-American mayor of Mt. Cedarmere. Talk about prestigious, right? Even when she was in college she was in politics, becoming President of the University of Maryland Student government Association. At the same time she was also captain of the mock trial team and the women's lacrosse team. How did she have time to sleep? Mayor Douglass inspired many girls like me to take on leadership roles, and because of her, I intend to run for student council next year. Ella said she would run with me and serve as vice president. We'll be a great addition to the school's political scene.

Everyone in town loves the mayor, too. She is always thinking of unique ways to bring the community together. She organized the Mt. Cedarmere 5K Fun Run and the Movie Night Under the Stars. People brought blankets and chairs to watch a movie on a gigantic screen in the park. She even started the Food Truck Grand Prix, which coincided with the Annual Mt. Cedarmere Fall Festival, a week-long carnival with concerts in the park. My family always participates in every event.

Mayor Douglass brushed her hair behind her shoulders and slid her tortoise shell eyeglasses up the bridge of her nose before adjusting the microphone stand to fit her height. She's not much taller than me! She cleared her throat, tapped the microphone with her finger to make sure it was on, and then held her hands out wide.

"Welcome, welcome, welcome to all the fine chefs of Mt. Cedarmere to the first ever Food Truck Grand Prix!"

Everyone applauded and cheered in unison.

"In just fifteen minutes, we will open the gates to allow the lovely citizens of Mt. Cedarmere to taste the delicious treats you have in store for them."

While Mayor Douglass addressed the crowd, I looked up at Pop Pop and could tell he was getting a little choked up again. I tugged at his sleeve. "Pop Pop?"

He wiped his tears away. "Sorry, Maddy, if your Pop Pop gets emotional today."

"It's okay, Pop Pop."

"But look around you. Look at all the wonderful people coming together, all the great chefs. It's a wonderful sight."

Today, would mean more than just winning to Pop Pop, but how could winning not be the main thing on his mind? Didn't he realize the other chefs were there to show him up? I may need to talk some sense into him.

"I agree, Pop Pop. However—"

The crowd roared, drowning out my voice.

"Ah, look, Maddy. Look, Cole! It's the trophy," Pop Pop cried, pointing to the stage.

Mayor Douglass held the trophy in one hand and a giant cardboard check in the other. "Along with the check for one thousand dollars, today's winner will receive this exquisite trophy."

The trophy was at least two feet tall and shinier than anything I'd ever seen. Shaped like a gigantic golden wine glass, like the ones my mom puts out for the holidays for the adults to drink from, the award had a bright emerald food truck mounted on the top. Cole and I looked at it with drool coming out of our mouths. "Wowwwwww."

"If that doesn't get you even more pumped to win today, Maddy, I don't know what will," Dad said.

He was right. I love trophies, but who doesn't?

As I mentally prepared to capture the trophy, I heard an obnoxious, high-pitched voice calling my name from behind me before someone tapped me on the shoulder. "Hey there, Maddy *Moooooo*."

I turned to find Kenny standing there with his arms crossed over his chest.

"Ugh...you. Hi, Kenny."

"Don't get too excited about that trophy. It may not have our names on it now, but it should, because it's practically ours even before this silly event starts."

"We'll see about that, Kenny."

"Oh, we will," he said. "If you get bored watching everyone pass by your truck on their way to my dad's, you can come over, and watch the band we'll have or the laser light show. Maddy, while you're serving up that slop you call food, we'll be rocking like celebrities on the red carpet."

It took all my restraint to keep from responding with equally snarky remarks. I wanted to, but my better judgment took over, and I refrained from adding fuel to his petty fire. I had to stay focused on my goal. Bickering back and forth with an arrogant kid like Kenny would only derail my motivation. Instead, I took the high road and stuck out my hand.

"Kenny, best of luck to you and your dad. You're a worthy competitor," I said, swallowing my pride and frustration.

"Eww, gross! Shake the hand of a loser like you? No way. I'll see you at the finish line, Maddy. We'll be the ones with the trophy held high and that pretty check in our hands."

A moment later, he was gone. Thankfully!

I put my arm around Cole. "Brother, don't worry about Kenny. That trophy and check are coming home with us today, not him."

Cole agreed.

"The rules are simple," Mayor Douglass continued. "When the guests arrive, they will be given a piece of paper with the list of every truck participating. At three o'clock, the competition will be over. All chefs must stop what they're doing and back away from the grill. Each community member will drop their vote into the collection box, and we will tally up the winner. The food truck with the most votes wins. Got it, chefs?"

"We got it, Mayor!" everyone sang.

"Good. No funny business. Now, when I blow this horn, it's time for you to get back to your trucks because the clock is ticking." She held a small air horn high above her head and counted down. "But before I do that, don't forget that the Mt. Cedarmere mayoral election will be coming back up soon, so remember: A vote for Douglass is a vote for Mt. Cedarmere!"

She paused and smiled for a few seconds without saying a word. Then one of her aids tapped her on her shoulder and whispered in her ear. "Okay, where were we..."

"You were about to start the competition!" someone shouted.

Mayor Douglass laughed. "Ah, yes. In that case, let's get this party started. In five, as in the number of months left before the election—four, three, two...ONE!" HOOOOOOONK went the air horn. It was time to get to work.

1, 2...3!

Take Your Places

Every team took off toward their trucks. My family rushed back to our truck as fast as we could, while Pop Pop did his best to hustle along with his cane. We immediately got into position. Dad would be the backup, helping with heavy items as Pop Pop cooked. He was also there if my mom needed something outside, while I took orders and organized meals with Pop Pop. Cole took his post with my mom outside, where they would help keep the customers in line or field questions about the menu. The latter was more of my mom's job, but Cole would try his best. Inside the truck, we got everything in place while Mom set up a table outside and put up a chalkboard displaying the specials.

"Mommy, you should use yellow to write the specials. It's bright and cheery," Cole said.

"And make it bold, too! You really want to draw them in," I added.

"You hear that, Reed?" Mom said. "Your daughter has quite the business mind."

My dad laughed and gave me the thumbs up. "Better listen to the boss, honey."

Pop Pop shuffled past me and Dad toward the front of the truck. Before stepping out, he waved us along. "Reed, Maddy, come with me."

"Pop Pop, where are you going? The event is starting any second," I said, putting the chips in order by flavor.

"Come, family, come together," he said again, waving his hands to gather everyone around outside. We all followed him to the picnic table my mom had set up. "I am so happy everyone came together to help out Pop Pop Fantastico today. It will be very busy today, so I will need everyone to help out and work together."

"Hey there, Pop Pop Fantastico."

"Ella, is that your voice I hear?" Dad asked while unwrapping a bag of French fries next to Pop Pop.

"Hi there, Mr. Perlman."

"I thought you were going to help us today?" Pop Pop asked.

"Oh, I am. And I will. I'm what you call a promoter. All of this was covered in the marketing book that Maddy and I got from the library. Chapter five is called 'How to Put the Pro in Promoter.' My job is to help bring people to the truck and trust me, I will deliver."

"I believe that."

"Watch how it works." Ella leaned closer and spoke softly so no one else could hear. "Ask me what I'd like to order, like we practiced."

"You got it. What can I help you with, young lady I've never seen before?" I asked.

Ella stepped back and raised her voice so everyone within earshot could hear her. "THAT'S SO NICE OF YOU TO ASK. YOU'RE BY FAR

THE NICEST FOOD TRUCK CHEF I'VE SEEN HERE ALL DAY."

"Ella, why are you yelling? That wasn't part of the plan."

"Just go with it," she said.

"Okay..." I frowned, feeling doubtful.

"I'LL HAVE A STACK OF YOUR FAMOUS CHOCOLATE CHIP PANCAKES. MMMM, DO I LOVE YOUR PANCAKES! DID I MENTION THEY WERE WORLD FAMOUS?"

"One order of pancakes coming up," I told Pop Pop.

"I hope your friend knows what she's doing," he said.

"Me, too."

"We'll call your name when it's ready. Thanks again for choosing Pop Pop Fantastico's."

"AND PLEASE TOSS ON TWO OF THOSE MADDY AND COLE COOKIES. I'LL TAKE ONE CHOCOLATE AND ONE VANILLA. MMMMM, THEY SURE LOOK DELICIOUS. IF THAT ISN'T THE BEST SERVICE I'VE EVER EXPERIENCED IN

MY WHOLE ENTIRE LIFE!" she blared. Then, she winked and stepped to the side to approach a mother with triplets that appeared to be around Cole's age.

"Excuse me, ma'am, it looks like your children could use a delicious breakfast," Ella said.

The woman appeared startled, but actually agreed with her. "Um, well...you're right. I mean, that is why we came to the Grand Prix today, isn't it?"

"It is! Might I suggest Pop Pop Fantastico's? I recently ordered a whole stack of pancakes myself. I'm sure your kids would love them too," she said, pressing her hand on the woman's back and urging her toward the ordering station. "Come on, kiddies. This way to some deliciousness!" she added, glancing at the woman's children.

"That does sound really good," the happy mother said.

"Hey, I'm glad to help out a lovely Mt. Cedarmere citizen. Maddy will help you out."

The woman made her way up to the window and both Pop Pop and Dad looked over at me in surprise. Ella's promotional work had been a success.

"She's pretty good, Maddy," Pop Pop said quietly.

"You're telling me."

The woman read the menu as Ella bowed in the background, congratulating herself on a job well done. She mouthed the words, "I'll be back soon with more people," then ran into the crowd.

"Welcome to Pop Pop Fantastico's," I said cheerily from the ordering station window. "How may I help you this fine morning?"

Pop Pop always said that you should greet each customer with a smile, a happy tone in your voice and an air of optimism, whether the day is clear or cloudy. I'd checked off all three. However, the customer didn't seem to care. Her kids were running around her as if she was a human merry-go-round.

"Kids, kids, kids, please give me five seconds! What do you want? Kids, what do you want?" she shouted, seeming very stressed out. Kind of like how my mom gets when Cole and I don't listen.

"Pancakes!" one shouted.

"Chocolate chip pancakes!" another screamed.

"Bagel and cream cheese!" said the third.

"Wait, so who wants what? Stop running around," she said, trying to corral them like a cowgirl catching a bunch of runaway piglets. "Oh gosh, I'm sorry, I don't remember what they wanted."

"Don't worry, we got it," Pop Pop said, peeking through the window beside me. "Isn't that right, Maddy?"

"Yup. Sure did. One stack of plain pancakes, one stack of chocolate chip, and one bagel with cream cheese. Would you like that bagel toasted?"

The mom was shocked. "Wow! You're good," she said, looking relieved.

"You know it!" Dad shouted from inside the truck as he began slicing the bagel.

"Yes, toasted," she added.

"That'll be $15.75, and my little brother, Cole—the one dancing like a goofball—will tell you when your meal is ready. It shouldn't be long." I leaned my head out the window and cupped my hands around my mouth to whisper. "I'll put an extra hustle on it for you, since I know the little ones will get antsy." Then I winked for good measure.

She smiled. "I really appreciate that."

I couldn't talk too long because another person was already waiting to order. It was my gym teacher, Mr. Styles.

"Good morning, Maddy."

"Hi, Mr. Styles. How can I help you on this super sunny day?"

"I've heard a lot about your Pop Pop's food truck, and I am looking for something that will fill my belly for a nice long workout later this morning."

"Say no more. I know exactly what you need." I turned to my dad and shouted, "One large bowl of Pop Pop's Protein-Packed Oatmeal Deluxe, please!"

"I love oatmeal," Mr. Styles said.

"Trust me, you'll really love this one. It has scrumptiously warm oatmeal topped with raisins, almonds, cocoa flakes, and drizzled with a perfect combination of honey and maple syrup.

If that doesn't scream autumn, then I don't know what does."

"That sounds delicious!"

A woman behind Mr. Styles raised her hand and said, "That does sound good. I'll take one, too."

"Make it a double, Dad!"

Man, this is going to be easy. I've really got the hang of this food truck business.

A third person in line called out, "I'll take an order of that, too!"

"I'll have a large stack of pancakes, chocolate chip!" a man said.

Now, the orders were flying in all directions, and I was beginning to get frustrated.

"What was that again?" I asked, trying to concentrate.

"Two eggs and a stack of pancakes!" another woman said.

"No, before that. Someone else wanted what?" My cheeks burned, and I felt flustered.

"Maddy, do you have this?" Pop Pop asked while he furiously worked the grill.

"I don't think so, Pop Pop. Everyone is yelling at the same time," I said, beginning to panic.

"Remember, take your time. This is your kitchen, your truck, and you control the flow," Pop Pop replied with confidence.

"I don't know if I can."

"You can do this, Maddy Moo," Dad offered. "This is your kitchen."

Mom was trying her best to calm the crowd, but everyone kept shouting their orders without waiting their turn. Even Mom began getting flustered.

"Patience, everyone! We'll get your orders soon," she said.

It seemed as if everything was moving in slow motion, as though time stood still, and I was trapped behind a glass wall just watching everyone yell.

Some of the customers waiting in line started to grumble.

A rude man in a big cowboy hat shouted, "Oh, come on, what kind of truck is this? All I want is some pancakes!"

More people rambled their orders like it was the floor of the stock market.

Pop Pop turned to me while plating the food. "Maddy, remember, this is your kitchen. You're the chef. Be the chef."

I took a deep breath and closed my eyes for a moment. I'm the chef. I control the kitchen. I'm the chef. I control the kitchen. I don't know what came over me, but finally, I'd had enough. It was time to take charge. I'm the chef. I control the kitchen. I walked out of the truck and into the crowd, put my hands on my hips and shouted, "WAIT A MINUTE!" The ground nearly trembled under my feet, and my face burned hot with emotion.

It worked.

The crowd froze and turned to face me. "People of Mt. Cedarmere, you MUST. CHILL. OUT! You're not animals, are you? You're adults. Let's act like adults. Trust me, you'll all get your food, but we must have order in the line." I smoothed the front of my jacket with the flat of my hand.

No one was sure how to respond, but one by one they started to nod. "Yeah, she makes a good point," someone said.

Another person murmured, "Maybe she's right..."

"Good," I said. "Now that we're on the same page, would anyone like some samples while they wait?" A flurry of hands shot up in the air. "Pop Pop, slice up some samples of our Maddy and Cole cookies for the fine people of Mt. Cedarmere."

"You heard that wonderfully powerful chef, Reed, didn't you?" Pop Pop said to my dad. "Grab a plate, and let's get those samples over there right away."

"On it, Pop Pop," Dad said.

"All right, all right, everyone. Form a line behind me," Cole said, boldly taking charge. "Or she'll come back out, and we don't want that to happen, do we?" The crowd played along with him, shaking their heads. "No one messes with my sister." He winked at me, and gave me a thumbs up. "I got ya, Moo."

86 The What?

After the initial fiasco of having to deal with the madhouse of impatient customers, the rest of the morning passed like a blur—a blur of food, money, smiles, and high fives. I didn't even notice any of the other trucks, nor did I worry about how they were doing. Sure, I saw people walk past our truck and to someone else's, but I couldn't focus on that; I had to worry about my work and keeping everyone happy. Before I knew it, it was already lunchtime and Pop Pop was prepping for sandwiches as the breakfast rush began to slow.

"We need more rye bread, Maddy!" Dad shouted while he worked on refilling the bread station.

"Eighty-six wheat bread, too," Pop Pop announced as he scurried past me to take Mrs. Maccabi's order for egg salad sandwich on toasted pumpernickel.

"Eighty-six?" I asked. "We have eighty-six slices left?"

"No, my dear, in the food industry the term *eighty-six* means it's gone. We are out of wheat bread."

"Oh, gosh! But everyone loves wheat bread," I said.

"Welcome to the food biz, Moo. We'll have to work around it. Remember, chefs must work on the fly. Trust me, there are worse things that can happen in the kitchen than running out of one kind of bread."

"Let your brother know, Maddy," Dad said.

Cole had been working all day, entertaining the customers with his unique dance moves and impressions of Buster the Buccaneer for anyone who cared to watch. I had to give the kid some credit. He had a lot of energy for a little guy who usually took a nap around this time. But he was cruising along like a veteran of the food service industry and didn't complain once.

"Coley! Eighty-six wheat bread. Spread the news, buddy."

"You got it, Maddy!" Cole said, rushing to the front of the line of customers.

"We have wheat bread sandwiches for eighty-six cents! That's right, eighty-six cents, folks! Come and get 'em!"

"What? No! Cole, it's not a sale! It means we're all out."

"Ohhhh. Well, why didn't you just say that?" he moaned. Cole put his hands up to his face to make his voice louder. "We're all out of sandwiches, folks. That's right, we're eighty-sixing the sandwiches." Then he winked back at me. "I got this, Moo."

I spoke too soon. "Ugh, no, you don't have it."

The crowd started to complain. "What, no sandwiches? I want a sandwich! If you guys are all out, I'll go somewhere else."

"No, no, no," I pleaded, half my body hanging out of the ordering window. "We are just out of wheat bread. We still have plenty of sandwiches, folks."

Thankfully, the crowd settled down again.

"You know, you guys sure are confusing sometimes," Cole said.

"Don't forget to vote for Pop Pop Fantastico's Fantastic Food Truck at the end of the day," Mom told the crowd. "We could use all your votes."

"That's right, my Pop Pop is the best Pop Pop around," Cole added.

"If only that was all it took to win," Pop Pop whispered before scooting by again with his cane.

"Oh, come on, Pop Pop, we got this thing in the bag," I told him.

"Maddy, my dear, never assume you've won until the referee raises your hand in victory. Remember my fight with the Hammer? Everyone thought he had won until the very last second— the last second—and then I came back. This fight is not over yet. Not even close."

I crinkled my nose. Way to be a party pooper, Pop Pop.

"He's right, Maddy," Dad said as he sliced the cucumbers into a silver bin next to the lettuce. "We have to work until the mayor sounds her horn, and then the votes are counted. You never know what surprise is waiting around the corner."

Just then, as if Dad had looked into the future, we heard a loud noise that rattled the entire truck. The sound was so deafening that it almost knocked items off the shelves and sent shivers through my body.

"What was that?" I asked, frightened.

Pop Pop leaned out of his seat and poked his head out the ordering window, looking around. "Up there." He pointed at a line of smoke in the clouds. Dad and I followed his gaze, our eyes widening in shock.

"What is that?" Mom asked.

"A fire across the park. Someone's truck is on fire!" Pop Pop said.

Rocking A Little Too Hard

The explosion caused panic and shouting. Cole hid behind my mom, trembling and clutching her leg. In front of our truck, people were dropping their meals and ducking to the ground, still uncertain what was going on. It only lasted a few seconds, but it had a huge effect on the event. We scurried out of the truck to see what was happening. On the other side of the park, flames leaped into the air. When I craned my neck, I could tell a truck wasn't actually on fire, but there was smoke everywhere around the truck, and it seemed to have started in the rear.

Pop Pop stuck his fingers in his ears, grimacing. "I think someone's generator exploded."

"That can happen?" I asked.

"If you're using too much power, it can," Dad said.

"Come on, we have to go help," Pop Pop said. "Sydney, Cole—you stay here, and watch the truck. We'll be back in a bit."

We hurried along to investigate.

As we made our way through the park, I could see where the smoke was coming from.

"That's Kenny's truck!" I shouted.

"Come on, Maddy, we have to go help!"

By the time we arrived, the fire department was attending to the small blaze. The generator looked like a little car engine on rubber wheels and reminded me of a lawn mower covered with buttons and knobs. A firefighter pulled it easily by the metal handle connected to the base, clearing it from the truck after she'd sprayed it with white foam to stop the fire. Since the generator had been placed behind the truck, not in or on it, the truck itself was safe. The thick electrical wire running to the side for about twenty feet looked like a black snake connecting two speakers, designed to support the band Kenny's dad had hired. At this point, nearly everyone at the Grand Prix had gathered around their truck.

Fire Chief Jordy wiped her sweaty brow with her sleeve. "All right, all right, show's over, folks—both mine and the band's. Boys..." She nodded to the three punk rock musicians. "You're done for the day." Then she addressed the crowd. "Mt. Cedarmere, we have it taken care of now."

Everyone applauded and cheered Fire Chief Jordy as if she was a gold medalist, and rightfully so.

Kenny's dad had his hands on his hips and kept shaking his head, terribly distraught over the accident, when Chief Jordy approached. "I don't know what happened, Chief."

"I do," she said.

"What's that?" Kenny asked, his face red from crying.

"You blew out your generator powering all your special effects and that over-the-top band.

The lights, the music, the speakers, all of it. Not only did you push everything to the max, but you made it erupt like a volcano," Chief Jordy said. "You may want to stick to just cooking and not trying to reenact Woodstock."

Mayor Douglass came running over, nearly out of breath. "What is going on here?" she exclaimed. "What is all the ruckus?"

"I'm so sorry," Kenny's dad said. "I had no idea, Mayor. I mean, I didn't think it would be too much. I guess I went overboard."

"You guess?" she asked pointedly. "I'd say you not only went overboard, but you have nearly sunk the entire ship!" She lifted the megaphone that was clipped to her hip, then addressed the crowd of people gathered around the food truck. "Okay, everyone, please go back to your stations. There is nothing to see here. The Food Truck Grand Prix must, and will, go on. We only have a couple of hours left and every vote counts!"

She turned to Kenny's dad. "Maybe not for you, though," she added.

Then she hustled back into the main center of the park where she continued to soothe shocked attendees.

Kenny held his dad's hand. "Does this mean we lost?" he asked, teary-eyed.

His dad put his arm around him. "I think so, son."

"Not today," Pop Pop said. "You are still in this fight."

Fight Fair

I tugged on Pop Pop's jacket. "What are you doing?"

"Maddy, we have to help your friend," he said.

"Whoa, wait a second. He's not my friend, Pop Pop. He's the town bully. Plus, now they're out of the competition, which makes our odds of winning even better."

Pop Pop tilted my chin up with his finger and shook his head. I could tell he was disappointed. "Is that really how you want to win?"

"What do you mean?" I asked.

"You want to win because someone else can't compete?"

"He's right," Dad said.

"But it's Kenny of all people," I replied, trying to reason with them.

Kenny was a mean bully who pushed me and our other classmates around. Why should we help him? What was I missing?

"Wouldn't you want someone's help if you were in their shoes?" Dad asked me.

"I would, but I guarantee Kenny wouldn't be the first in line to assist." I shrugged.

"That's not the point, Maddy."

"A real chef helps other chefs in need," Pop Pop added. "Aren't you a real chef?"

I nodded.

I started to realize where I'd gone wrong.

"I am a real chef. But what I meant was..."

Pop Pop leaned down to my level and met my eyes. "Maddy, if we want to take home the trophy and award for having the best food truck in town, we have to make sure that it's fair. Remember when I beat the Hammer?"

"Of course."

"I beat him at his best, not while he was weak or sick. And that is what made my victory worth it. If he simply forfeited his title or fought with a broken arm, I wouldn't have truly won anything. Do you follow?"

"Yes, Pop Pop. If Kenny can't compete, we'll never know who is the best," I said, finally understanding.

Pop Pop kissed my cheek. "Exactly, kiddo," he said proudly.

"But how can we help? I mean, they're out of power? Does your magic also mean you can shoot some electricity back into their generator?"

"Not exactly, but I have an idea..."

Friends, Enemies, and Frenemies

Pop Pop hobbled over to Kenny's dad. "Sir, my name is Pop Pop Fantastico."

"I'm Gary," said Kenny's dad, who was still very upset.

Kenny rudely interrupted, sneering at me. "What? Did you come over to rub it in my face that we can't compete anymore, Maddy?"

"Kenny!" Gary snapped. "Don't say that."

"Actually, we're here to help you, Mr. Know-It-All," I told him with a nice touch of attitude. I felt it was deserved.

"She's right," Pop Pop added.

Gary scratched his head. "Wait, so you'd risk losing the event? This is your free pass to the gold trophy, Mr. Fantastico."

Pop Pop straightened his back and tilted his chin up, looking very proud. "Pop Pop Fantastico does not take free passes."

I smiled and crossed my arms, feeling equally gratified. Take that, Kenny!

"Gary, I have a small backup generator that you can use if you like. It's nothing fancy, and it won't be able to run your light show or hold another concert, but it will allow you to cook for the next couple of hours and finish the Grand Prix. Your ovens are still hot, the fridges and freezers are still cold. If you agree, we can have you back up in five minutes, and it will be as if you never missed a beat."

As much as I disliked Kenny, and despite him being so mean to me all the time, I did feel bad for him. Friend or not, this was a terrible accident. Even worse, I always got upset when I saw other kids cry in public. Most kids think it's tough to hide their emotions, but not me. Pop Pop always said, "When you're upset, you have to let it out, or it will boil up like soup on a hot stove." It's hard to think about soup at a time like this, but Pop Pop was right then, too. I knew how hard it was for Kenny—who had a reputation for being a tyrant—to cry in front of everyone, so I could only imagine the pain he was feeling at that moment. It must have been very upsetting to him, and no one deserved to feel that way.

Gary thought for a moment, then looked down at Kenny. "What do you think, son? Would you like to keep going?"

Kenny smiled. "Totally, Dad!"

Gary stuck out his hand to Pop Pop. "You are a true gentleman, Pop Pop Fantastico. Regardless of who wins, I will be sure to let everyone know how kind you were today."

"It's a deal. Let's shake on it." Pop Pop smiled, and the two men shook hands.

"Kenny, what do you say to Maddy for helping us out? I believe you owe her a thank you, at the very least."

Kenny sheepishly stepped forward, his chin buried into his chest. "Thank you, Maddy," he mumbled.

"Speak up, son," Gary demanded.

Kenny slowly lifted his head. "Thank you, Maddy."

"No problem, Kenny."

"And..."

"And what?" I asked.

He took a deep breath. "And...I'm sorry for picking on you in school."

What? Was this really happening? Was the biggest, meanest bully in the entire history of our school actually apologizing to me? I was more shocked by this than I had been by the explosion. Part of me did want to rub it in, but that would be tacky. I was better than that.

"No worries, Kenny. I'm glad you guys can still participate today."

"Me, too."

"So, friends?" I asked, extending my hand.

Kenny's eyes lit up like the truck's fancy neon signs before their generator exploded. "You'd want to be friends with me?"

"Sure, but only if you promise not to push kids around or act like you're better than everyone else."

Kenny agreed. "It's a deal, friend."

Pop Pop clapped his hands together. "Okay, great. We have an agreement. Kenny, how about you go tell the mayor you're still involved, while Gary and I go get the generator."

"Kenny, wait. I'll go with you," I said.

"Thanks, Maddy," Kenny replied, smiling.

When The Hippos Sing

After we helped wheel the generator over to Kenny and his dad, we immediately got back to work. Cole and my mom were in front of our truck, helping clean up the mess people made when they dropped their food during the big bang from the generator. Pop Pop and I hurried back into the truck and took our positions. He leaned on his cane by the grill, and I stood next to my dad by the window to help take orders. It was clear that my dad had been working hard while Pop Pop and I were gone. He hadn't missed a beat!

"I have fresh tomatoes and pickles sliced. I'll refill the condiments and clean out a few of the bowls, chefs," Dad said.

"Ah, great work, my boy!" Pop Pop said.

"Ditto, Daddy."

"You hear that, Maddy?" Pop Pop asked.

"Hear what?"

"Your dad said, 'chefs,' as in plural, not 'chef' as in only me."

"That's right, Pop Pop," Dad said. "I said chefs because I'm looking at two chefs, not one."

Then my dad kissed the top of my head. "That was very brave and very kind, what you did to help Kenny. A good chef cares for others and encourages them to always try. I love you, Maddy Moo."

"Thanks, Daddy. That really means a lot to me," I said, hugging him back.

"We got a full house over here. A big ole full house," Cole shouted from outside to us.

"Let's get their orders going, folks," I said excitedly.

"Maddy, it looks like we sold out of Maddy and Cole cookies, too. Wow, they were a hit!" Dad said.

"We sold out?" I gasped.

I can't believe my idea was such a hit. My cookies, made from scratch, all sold out? I couldn't let people down. I needed to meet the demand.

"We need more. I have to bake more."

"Don't worry, sweetie," Pop Pop said. "There will be plenty of time to sell more cookies. They'll come back for more. Trust me, they always do. Now's not the time to worry about that."

"All right, people, let's go. Whip out that money and make sure you vote for my Pop Pop. It's not over until the fat hippo sings," Cole said, which made the entire line burst out laughing.

"I think the expression is, 'It's not over until the fat lady sings,' Cole," my mom said.

"Mommy, it's not nice to call anyone fat. That could hurt their feelings. But hippos don't care, so it's cool," he said, as if it should be obvious to everyone.

"Hey, he's got a point," I said.

"Okay, Coley," Mom laughed. "Hippos it is."

The incident with the generator didn't slow down the crowd, and we were back to doing what we did best. Ella continued to direct traffic our way, while Mom ushered them into line and helped with the menu. Cole entertained onlookers with dances and songs. Inside the truck, I was taking orders, stacking sandwiches high, filling drinks, and making people smile...exactly like a real chef.

Three... Two... One

Time was moving fast. "One more minute, gang!"
Mom shouted, looking at her watch. "One more
minute until the Grand Prix is over."

"One more minute?" I asked, while handing
my neighbor, Mr. Bennett, his turkey sandwich.
"It feels as if Mayor Douglass's fifteen minute
warning was only fifteen seconds ago."

"Well, now it's fifty-five seconds!" she said.

"We're down to the wire!" I yelled to Pop Pop.

"Remind everyone to hand in their votes after
the horn," he said.

"Ah, you're right. I almost forgot." I cupped my
hands around my mouth. "There are only a few

seconds left in the day. Please make sure to hand in your vote for Pop Pop Fantastico's Fantastic Food Truck!"

My mom went around reminding everyone to turn in their votes before they left, while handing out coupons for their next visit.

Then, the mayor's voice could be heard over the megaphone. "Let's hear it, Mt. Cedarmere. Fifteen, fourteen, thirteen—"

"Maddy, Reed, let's go outside and count down together," Pop Pop said.

"It's over?" I asked.

"No, Maddy," Pop Pop said, taking my hand in his. "It's only just begun. Now, come, we have only ten seconds left."

Pop Pop, Daddy, Mommy, Cole and I gathered in a circled together, holding hands and counting along with the Mayor.

"Ten, nine, eight, seven..." With each number, we got louder and louder. "Six, five, four, three, two...one!"

Mayor Douglass's air horn blared like my Uncle Chase's pet beagle, Camden, whenever he howled at someone ringing the doorbell. That sound officially ended the Grand Prix. When we heard the horn, relief set in, and we were all completely drained. I looked at Pop Pop, who looked back at me. We glanced at Dad, and as if a giant boulder had been lifted off our backs, we all collapsed from exhaustion, right there on the ground. We could have landed in a pile of mud, for all I cared. We needed it. I had never worked so hard in my entire life, and that included the time Ella and I once mowed five lawns in one afternoon, trying to earn enough money for new Rollerblades.

Pop Pop was the first to rise, digging his cane into the ground for support.

"Come now, crew," he said, grabbing my hand. "Now, we celebrate."

I stood up with help from Pop Pop. "Celebrate? Celebrate what? We didn't win yet."

"Yes, but we tried our best and that's the real victory."

"Maybe in your world, Pop Pop, but I really wish trying came with the same payday as winning does."

Pop Pop erupted into laughter. "You sure are one smart cookie, Maddy Moo."

"Like my Maddy and Cole cookies. Man, Pop Pop, we really crushed it today with them. I think we have something there."

"Um, hello? Is anyone going to help me up?" said Dad, who was still sprawled out on the ground like a marionette whose strings had been cut.

"Oh, Daddy, come here, you big baby." I pulled him to his feet, with every last bit of strength I had left, even though I'm pretty sure he could have done it himself.

"Wasn't that fun?" Pop Pop asked.

"Fun? I think I may need two months of physical therapy to fix my back. When I used to help Pop Pop fifteen years ago, my body was in much better shape," Dad teased.

"It was more than fun, Pop Pop," I said. "I wish I could do this every day!"

Pop Pop winked at me.

"I wish I could dance every day, too," Cole added.

"That you can definitely do, sweetie boy," Mom told him.

"Put your hands in the middle, one more time before we head to the award ceremony," Pop Pop said. "We have some time while Mayor Douglass's team tallies the votes."

"On the count of three, I want to hear you shout '*Fantastico!*' so everyone can hear," Pop Pop said. On three, we screamed so loud, we were sure everyone knew our name.

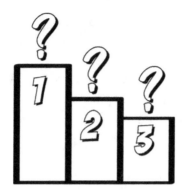

It All Comes Down To This

We walked like zombies, in slow, sluggish movements, conserving every last ounce of energy, to the award ceremony which was being held where Mayor Douglass had kicked off the Grand Prix. As it was when we'd started, the glowing trophy and check was on display, teasing us the same way it had after the unveiling. Every food truck employee was represented and nearly every citizen in Mt. Cedarmere was in attendance, too. Mayor Douglass took the stage, relishing her time in the spotlight. She held an envelope in her hand, which held my future inside.

She stretched her arms wide. "What a day, what a day, what a day!"

We all cheered.

"I think we'll have to do this every year. Am I right?" she said.

Again, we cheered.

"First, I'll need to fix my back," Dad said, wincing.

"Before we worry about next year, let's focus on what you're all here for," Mayor Douglass said. "Who will be this year's Charm City Food Truck Grand Prix winner?"

Pop Pop had his arms around me and Cole. "Fingers crossed, little ones."

"And your toes," Cole said.

"I would be nervous, if I still had feeling in my body," Dad said.

"People of Mt. Cedarmere, it appears you had a very tough decision to make. Based on your votes, it was a very tight race," Mayor Douglass announced. "It came down to only one vote separating the winner from the rest of the pack."

"Oh no, Pop Pop. It's soooooooo close," I said in agony.

The mayor cleared her throat. "Okay, now I will open the envelope and see who the big winner is." She started to tear the corner and it felt like an eternity. Each millisecond of the paper ripping felt like years off my life.

Come on, Mayor Douglass, do it faster. Faster! Like a Band-Aid—one pull, RIP!

Finally, after two agonizing seconds, the envelope was opened and she pulled out a card. She scanned the crowd. "Who will it be? Whose name is on this card? Who takes home the grand prize?"

"Tell us already!" Cole blurted out.

"Settle down, settle down, everyone. This is called building the suspense," she said.

People were getting restless, and Mayor Douglass could tell no one enjoyed her humor.

"Well, the suspense is killing us!" shouted Scott from Scooter's Gyro Truck.

"Yeah, just tell us!" said Irene from Irene's Ice Cream Trailer.

"Geez. Fine. Thought I'd make this a bit more interesting for you," she said, sighing. "But I get it."

"Here we go, team," Mom said as she and my dad hugged Pop Pop.

"And the winner of the first ever Mt. Cedarmere Food Truck Grand Prix is..."

The crowd fell so silent it was as if everyone's voices had been taken from their bodies. Then, suddenly, things started to move in slow motion. I saw Mayor Douglass's lips move, but I couldn't hear the words coming out of her mouth. Like before, my emotions were so overwhelming it felt like I was trapped, completely incapable of separating reality from fantasy. Was I really hearing her announce the winner? Would all of my hard work come down to this one moment? Then, as if I was in the ocean watching a wave roll toward me, I closed my eyes and let Mayor Douglass's words wash over me.

In an instant, my life changed forever.

"Pop Pop Fantastico's Fantastic Food Truck!" Mayor Douglass roared into the microphone.

Wait, is this a dream?

"We won, Maddy! We did it!" Pop Pop screamed.

My mom picked up Cole and my dad pulled me into his arms. "Let's go, Moo! Let's go get our award!"

I was still in shock. It wasn't until we were on stage with the mayor that I realized what was happening. I had never met the mayor in person before. Now, she was handing me a check for one thousand dollars—way more money than I'd ever seen in my life—and Pop Pop was holding a trophy. Just as I was beginning to wrap my brain around all the excitement, Mayor Douglass pushed the microphone toward me.

I froze.

"Maddy, say something to the crowd," Mayor Douglass told me.

I still couldn't believe it.

My dad whispered in my ear, "We won, Maddy. The mayor wants you to say something."

"Me?" I asked, my voice echoing over the crowd.

"Yes, you, darling," Mayor Douglass replied. "Pop Pop Fantastico's Fantastic Food Truck won the Grand Prix."

I scanned the crowd and all of Mt. Cedarmere. Everyone stared back at me waiting for me to say something. I saw Ella, her brother Noah, Mrs. Mechak, my school principal, kids from my lacrosse and basketball team, neighbors, classmates, as well as Kenny. Everyone looked at me. They looked so happy, as if they, too, had won the prize. I made eye contact with Ella and saw her mouth the words, "We did it, Maddy!" Her words had some sort of magical spell which snapped me back to life.

"We did it," I said softly in the microphone.

"You sure did," Mayor Douglass said.

All of Mt. Cedarmere started clapping for me.

"We did it!" I shouted into the microphone, feeling more energized than ever.

"That's the spirit," Mom said, tapping my shoulders.

My confidence was alive and well. Suddenly, I felt like a rock star on stage. I grabbed the microphone and paced across the stage. "We did it!" I yelled. "Pop Pop Fantistico's Fantastic Food Truck did it, Mt. Cedarmere!"

The audience clapped again and just like they did for Pop Pop when he beat the Hammer, they started chanted, "Fantastico! Fantastico! Fantastico!"

Today belongs to the underdogs, I thought.

"Never underestimate the power of an underdog. Isn't that right, Pop Pop?" I said.

Mom, Dad, Cole, and Pop Pop joined me and Mayor Douglass for a photo from Mt. Cedarmere Daily News. The flashes from the cameras came so rapidly, I wasn't even sure if I was smiling or not. I had never been in the paper before, and now, we were officially famous.

"Give it up, one more time for Pop Pop Fantistico!" Mayor Douglass said.

As we were walking off the stage, Gary and Kenny met us at the steps.

"We wanted to congratulate you and Maddy on a job well done, Pop Pop Fantastico. I can't thank you enough for your help earlier," Gary said.

"My pleasure, Gary. I know you would have done the same," Pop Pop said.

"I hope I have the chance to pay it forward one day. Pop Pop, if you ever need anything, please don't hesitate to call. I'll see you next year at the Grand Prix," he said with a grin.

"Ah, the competition already begins, Gary," Pop Pop replied jokingly. "May the best team win."

"Today, the best team did win, Pop Pop," Kenny said. "That's why we voted for you. Me, my dad, our entire family and the staff."

I scratched my head. "You voted for us? Why wouldn't you vote for yourselves?"

"The rules said to vote for your favorite food truck, and we did," Kenny said.

"That's very kind of you, Kenny," Mom told him.

He smiled sheepishly and started to blush.

"You fought a good fight today, Kenny. I'll see you in school on Monday, buddy."

We started back to Pop Pop's truck to pack up, and Dad gave me a playful nudge. "I think Kenny likes you, Moo."

"Eww, gross! Are you serious? Three hours ago, he was my worst enemy in the history of our school. Let's not get ahead of ourselves here."

Ugh—the very thought!

Livin' The Dream

We said our good-byes to the other food trucks around the park, and everyone congratulated us on the big win. I knew they respected Pop Pop as a chef, but after today, it catapulted him into legendary status amongst the other chefs. Pop Pop may not have said it, but I know it meant a lot to him. During the ride home, I couldn't get the smile off my face. Pop Pop let me take the trophy home and the check as well. We strapped the trophy down with a seat belt between me and Cole. Cole fell asleep in his car seat, one hand still on the trophy. I couldn't even think about sleeping. How can I sleep when my dream is now a reality?

We each took a bath and got ready for bed. Cole was practically falling asleep while my mom brushed his teeth. The trophy sat next to my bed. Tucker snuggled with his favorite toy beside it and fell asleep, as well. I pulled the covers up to my chin and put my hands behind my head. Today was unbelievable. After Cole went to bed, my parents came into my room to say good night.

Mom and Dad sat next to each other by my side.

"It meant a lot to Pop Pop, and to us, to see you out there today," Dad said proudly.

"So, Moo, what's next?" Mom asked.

"According to that big check over there, a new bike," I said.

"She's right, Reed. She did exactly what we asked and then some."

"Yup. Deal's a deal, sweetie. Tomorrow, we'll get the bike." Dad gave me a high five. "You really stepped up like a pro today, kiddo."

"You should be spent. Get some sleep. Me and your dad are going to do the same."

After they left, I walked to my window and looked at the stars, just as I do every night before bed. I looked at the sky, then pulled the curtain across my window. "Sorry, stars, there's no need to wish on you tonight," I said to the darkness. "I'll think of a new dream and then get back to you."

I rubbed Tucker's ears and got back to into bed. "For now, I'll enjoy my dream coming true."

Maddy & Cole's Fantastic Food Truck

Before getting my new bike, I had to work on a school project about my favorite U.S. president, which was due on Monday. Of course, I waited until the last minute, but after I was done, we would go bike shopping. Cole sat at the kitchen table next to me, drawing with crayons, as I placed cotton balls onto a piece of construction paper to make George Washington's hair. As I placed the last cotton ball on his head, I heard the deep sound of a car horn blaring in the driveway.

I'd know that honk anywhere.

"Pop Pop!" Cole and I sang.

We ran outside, Mom and Dad not far behind us with Tucker on his leash.

"*La mia famiglia*," Pop Pop said, arms open, as he leaned on the truck's bumper. We were nearly blinded by the light reflecting off Pop Pop's truck, which was a first.

"Wow, Pop Pop, your truck is so clean," I said.

"It's like glitter," Cole said.

"Lookin' good, Pop Pop." Dad nodded.

Pop Pop took out his handkerchief and rubbed a small spot off the headlight. "You know, I don't like change very much but cleaning this truck up a bit is a good change."

"Did you stay up all night?" Mom asked.

"Cleaning? No, that I took care of at the car wash this morning. Turns out the owner was at the Grand Prix yesterday and gave me a free coat of wax! How do you like that?"

"Get used to being a local celebrity, Pop Pop," I said.

"To answer your question, there was something else I worked on all night. Here, come to the side of Pop Pop's truck," he said, leading us to a large bed sheet with the top corners taped to his truck. "Cole and Maddy, when I say 'now,' I want you to pull this sheet."

"Okay..." I said curiously.

Cole looked at me and giggled.

"I know that Pop Pop's truck needed a wash, but after yesterday, it was missing something other than just a scrubbing." He put his hand on his chin, then tapped his cheek with his finger. "Pop Pop started thinking, and I decided to make a change."

"What kind of change?" I asked.

"You'll see...Right...NOW!"

Following his command, we pulled the sheet off and he was right; there was a change for sure. A very, very big change.

"Is that me?" Cole said.

Pop Pop nodded.

"And is that me?" I asked.

"Wait, you changed the name, too?" Dad asked.

"What does it say? What does it say?" Cole asked impatiently.

"That's right. Can you please read it out loud, Maddy?" Pop Pop asked me.

"Dad, did you do this yourself?" Mom asked, covering her mouth with one hand.

"Pop Pop, you are a man of many talents," Dad added.

"Well, it's a little rough. And due to my leg, I had to take many breaks. So later this week, I'm bringing it to Mr. Feirstein's body shop to freshen it up and make it really POP."

I looked back at my mom and dad to make sure I wasn't dreaming this as well, since the past twenty-four hours had been a whirlwind of things that were never supposed to come true.

"Go ahead, Maddy. Read it," Cole said, flailing his hands, unable to contain himself.

Pop Pop's old logo had been painted over with a new image and the new name of his truck. I took a deep breath and said, "It says, Maddy and Cole's Fantastic Food Truck."

"Those are our names!" Cole screamed. "Is this our truck?"

Not only was the name changed, but instead of the old paint that had been steadily chipping off the truck, there was a caricature of me and Cole in our chefs' coats with Pop Pop's arms around us and his head between us both. In one hand, I had a plate full of pancakes with syrup drizzled on top, and the other hand presented a fresh baked chocolate Maddy and Cole cookie. Cole was making a funny face—of course—while holding a thick bagel sandwich on a plate.

"It is." Pop Pop turned to me. "Do you like it?" he asked, his voice cracking with emotion. Overwhelmed with pride and love for his family, Pop Pop's voice reflected his current mood.

"Do I like it? I mean, look at it! How could I not like it?"

I hugged Pop Pop tighter than ever.

"Maddy, I'll take that as a 'yes.'"

"Big time yes," I told him.

"This is the truck I've always wanted," Pop Pop began. "You can take all the expensive, fancy trucks in the world, but all mine needed was some inspiration. That means the world to me."

Pop Pop wiped away another tear. "Oh, gosh, you know Pop Pop gets emotional."

"We all are," Mom said.

Pop Pop wiped his eyes with his handkerchief. "Well, I know you're going to get your new bike now, so I don't want to hold you up, but I wanted to make sure you saw this right away. Pop Pop is going to the softball fields off Shawan Road. There is a big tournament today by the Oregon Ridge Park, which means there will be a lot of hungry athletes. I need to get a good spot to show off the new truck."

"I still can't get over it, Pop Pop. This is way better than a bike," I said, still astonished by his gesture.

"Really?" Dad asked. "Because I'm pretty sure the bike is all you've talked about for the past few weeks."

"And now you earned it. In fact, I can get a bike rack for the truck, if you'd like?" Pop Pop suggested.

I thought for a moment.

"Maddy? Would you like Pop Pop to get the bike rack?" he asked again.

I remained silent.

I walked closer to the truck and ran my hands across the logo. Then, I traced the tires and the grill with my fingers taking in the entirety of Pop Pop's new and improved truck.

"We could use brighter headlights, Pop Pop," I said. "I read online about these new headlights that are ten times brighter than normal head-lights and can save your battery life."

"Sure. I can consider that, I guess," Pop Pop said.

"And the tires."

"What about them, dear?" Mom asked.

"Mr. Bryson over at Bryson Tires has a sale coming up in two weeks. He was telling me about it during the Grand Prix. I think he would be will-ing to offer us tires for a good price. If we're going to get the winter crowds during the snowy days, we'll need good tires."

"Yes. We could do that, too...one day," Pop Pop said, unsure of what I was leading up to.

"We can also sell our t-shirts. I can't tell you how many times people complimented me on our new shirts. Mrs. Keane's Print Shop, who did our shirts, told me they'd be happy to work with us again. I'll talk to her about buying in bulk. My book mentioned that's a good way to get a better price."

"Oh, I don't know. T-shirts are very expensive," Pop Pop said, seeming worried.

I folded my arms, then rubbed my chin as if I had a beard. "Also in my business book it mentions having a social media strategy. People can track us wherever we go and see photos of our adventures on their phone. It's a mobile world, Pop Pop, and we have to get in the game."

"I still have one of those flip phones." Pop Pop said, showing us his practically ancient cell phone.

"We'll need to upgrade you then."

"A new phone?" he asked.

"Yes, and launch an online system to allow customers to place orders in advance. We'll need a laptop at least, with Wi-Fi access. Mine works well, but you should have one, too. My book said we should ask if any stores have small business offerings. It's a thing, Pop Pop."

"A computer? Pop Pop is not good with computers, Maddy. I don't know about that."

"But I am. In fact, I can help out a lot more with the business than just the food prep."

"Maddy, these ideas are wonderful, they really are, but I don't think Pop Pop can afford all the projects you have in mind," Mom said.

"Yes, he can." I leaned against the truck and placed my hands on my hips. "I think we could easily get them done."

"Maybe over time," Pop Pop said. "Not all at once, though."

"What if we use our winnings?"

"The winnings are for your new bike," Dad said.

I waved my hand. "Nah, the bike can wait. I can always find another one that's just as good and a lot less expensive. After all, I'd much rather use my money for an investment."

"Investment?" Pop Pop asked.

"That's in my business book, too."

Pop Pop put his arm around me. "Maddy, I appreciate your help, but you earned that money. That was the deal we had, and I can't ask you to give it back."

"Pop Pop's right, Maddy. You went way beyond your goal," Dad added.

"Last time I checked that win was a family effort, not just mine. Dad was hustling like crazy, Pop Pop was working on one leg, Mom directed traffic, and Cole went nap-free to make us win—not just me. Ella lost her voice screaming for us. A bit much, but it was an effort. Seems like the money would be better spent in our family truck than for a bike I don't really need."

"Sydney, check my pulse, because I can't be alive right now," Dad said, thrusting his arm toward my mom. "You drove us bonkers about this bike, Maddy, so we offered a challenge. You completed the challenge, and after all that, you want to give it back?"

"I can't give it back if it wasn't mine to begin with."

"Maddy, what are you saying?" Pop Pop asked.

"I'm saying that Pop Pop built this truck with his bare hands, not with magic, but with a dream. He was an underdog when he defeated the Hammer, and we were underdogs when we won the Grand Prix. Like his match, we believed in ourselves yesterday and I believe even more in this food truck—more now than ever. Plus, in my business book it talks about franchising, which means having many trucks, not just one. I need to start my empire ASAP."

Everyone laughed with me.

"An empire?" Mom asked.

"Sure, why not? We gotta to start somewhere."

Pop Pop threw his hands in the air. "*La mia famiglia!* Come dance with me. Come, come," he said, holding his hands out to us.

We joined him in a small circle in our driveway, and even Tucker got involved. "*Il future*, Maddy and Cole. *Il future!* That means 'the future', my dear. To the future of Maddy and Cole's Fantastic Food Truck."

I slipped away from the group and jumped into the driver's seat of the truck, then leaned down with all my might and honked the horn twice before hollering out the window, "How many more years until I get to drive this bad boy myself, Mom?"

"You have some time. Don't get too excited," she said.

"Fine, fine. It doesn't matter. We have many more journeys before then. There's another competition in Bethany Beach in November, so we'd better get planning. Come on, Cole. Let's go, Pop Pop. The road is calling us. Hold on tight! We are in for quite an adventure...and it's only just begun."

About the Author

Richie Frieman is a best selling, award winning author and illustrator. His success spans multiple literary genres and includes launching an online music magazine. Several of Frieman's written works have been featured in major print publications nationally and internationally.

Along with his literary pursuits, Frieman has had an adventurous career as a professional artist, inventor, clothing designer, entrepreneur, and wrestler. He spent eight years wrestling professionally and won over a dozen titles in various federations throughout the U.S. Frieman's fascinating background has led to several live appearances on media outlets across the globe.

He is a proud graduate of the University of Maryland, College Park where he earned a degree in Fine Arts. Frieman currently lives in Owings Mills, Maryland with his wife, Jamie, their two children, Maddy and Cole, and their precocious puppy, Tucker.

For more on Richie Frieman, please visit his website: www.richiefrieman.com

CPSIA information can be obtained
at www.ICGtesting.com
Printed in the USA
FSHW04n0036120418
46623FS